THE NIGHT RIDERS

After pulling off one of the greatest cattle drives in history, Wade Jericho is a hero to the townsfolk of Trail's End. But Wade has brought with him some notorious gunslingers, former Union soldiers to a man. These desperadoes intend to take over and destroy what was once a Confederate town. Then, Trail's End is suddenly raided by the infamous Night Riders. Marshal John Prayer, young and inexperienced, will have to stand alone against them all.

1

THE Night Riders came galloping hard out of the sunset across the plain. They entered the town screaming and shooting. There were a dozen of the invaders, wearing long white dusters over their clothes, with kerchiefs masking their faces. Four of the riders were carrying blazing torches of wood wrapped in cloth and soaked in pitch. The others fired their Colts and Winchesters wildly into the stores and houses on either side of the street.

In their first headlong rush they galloped unchallenged past the livery stable. Two of the men hurled their torches into the bales of straw spilling out on to the street. The tinder-dry material exploded into spitting tongues of fire which almost at once rose and flickered round the framework of the

1

stable. Soon the whole building was engulfed in roaring flames. Two more of the riders threw their blazing torches on to the boardwalk lining the street.

The Night Riders rode on, deep into the heart of the small town, their guns cocked to shoot down any panic stricken inhabitants as they fled in disorder. But no one appeared. The leading rider reined his mount to a halt and jerked his head from side to side in the gloom. He was controlling his horse with one hand. In the other he carried easily the flag of the anti-slavery Night Riders of Kansas, a yellow star against a pale blue background

"There's no one here!" yelled another rider, jostling his mount up close. "Where the hell are they?"

Comprehension and fury writhed agonizingly across the face of the leader, just as the first rifle shots crackled from the windows and roofs of the stores on either side of the main street, sending two of the Night Riders at once toppling and screaming from

JEFF KINCAID

THE NIGHT RIDERS

Complete and Unabridged

LINFORD
Leicester

First published in Great Britain in 1996 by
Robert Hale Limited
London

First Linford Edition
published 1997
by arrangement with
Robert Hale Limited
London

The right of Jeff Kincaid to be identified as
the author of this work has been asserted
by him in accordance with the
Copyright, Designs and Patents Act, 1988

British Library CIP Data

Kincaid, J. D.
    The night riders.—Large print ed.—
Linford western library
    1. Western stories
    2. Large type books
    I. Title
823.9'14 [F]

ISBN 0-7089-5133-3

Published by
F. A. Thorpe (Publishing) Ltd.
Anstey, Leicestershire

Set by Words & Graphics Ltd.
Anstey, Leicestershire
Printed and bound in Great Britain by
T. J. International Ltd., Padstow, Cornwall

This book is printed on acid-free paper

their rearing mounts.

"It's a trap!" he yelled. "They've been waiting for us!"

The other riders swore and wrestled with their frightened horses in confusion as the deadly fusillade poured into their ranks, sending more of the invaders crashing bleeding and dying to the ground.

Above the scene of sudden destruction three of the leading townsfolk were sprawled on the flat roof of the saloon, overlooking the main street. Marshal Tod Washburn was discharging his Henry rifle with casual but deadly accuracy into the threshing group of horsemen below. On either side of him Kennedy, the saloon owner, and Ellcott, the proprietor of the town's provender store, were wrestling with considerably less accuracy with their own firearms. Sweat rolled down their faces as they tried to match the lethal firepower of the lawman. For a second Ellcott stopped and goggled over the edge at the carnage below.

"Keep firing, damn you!" roared Washburn at him. "This is the only chance we're going to get. If we let them get away from the main street they'll scatter and come up behind us and pick us off."

His warning was all that was necessary. Ellcott and Kennedy started to blast away again. Washburn grunted in satisfaction and turned and squirmed his way across to the trap-door in the roof leading down to the saloon.

"I'm going down to the street," he grunted.

For a moment the marshal paused to see if the next part of his plan was being put into operation. He nodded with satisfaction when he saw that it was. As the deadly fusillade of shots continued from both sides of the thoroughfare, at the end of the street from which the riders had entered, by the blazing livery stables, a group of storekeepers and cowboys, led by Steve Johnson, the owner of the hardware store, with Doc Ember, the town's nearest approach to a medical practitioner, close behind him, suddenly dragged three carts loaded with sacks of grain across the street and abandoned them, before scuttling back to their shelters, effectively blockading the exit from the town.

The leader of the Night Riders stared desperately at the other end of the street. For the first time through the gloom he saw the impenetrable piles of timber which had been assembled earlier that day to complete the trap. His desperate, searching eyes saw that the ambush had been prepared with meticulous care. Every possible avenue of escape had been blocked off well in advance. The townsfolk pouring their shots down were so well hidden that it was impossible to shoot back with any certainty of hitting a man. With a sinking heart the leader realized that only one man in the area could have planned and carried out such a deadly reception, and that man almost certainly was looking down at him from somewhere with grim satisfaction now.

The townsfolk, hidden in the buildings, continued to fire their rifles and revolvers in volley after volley on the milling group of riders caught below them. One person in the street was not armed. From his hideout behind an upturned rocking chair of Mrs Richmond's boarding house, a ten-year old boy watched the bloody action with horrified fascination. He saw the survivors of the first onslaught of bullets looking desperately for their attackers hidden in the night and firing wildly into the darkness.

The boy dug in deeper behind his chair, half-terrified, half-awed at the sight. Earlier that night he had crept out of bed and climbed down into the street, using several knotted sheets from his bed, to get a worm's eye view of the ambush he had heard his elders talking so much about over the past few days. Only a few yards away from him the survivors of the raid were huddled close together, looking with little hope to their leader for salvation.

"What are we going to do, Clem?" screamed one of the Night Riders, thrashing his sweating horse next to the mount of the leader.

"Only thing we can do," shouted Clem hoarsely. "Ain't no way out. We'll take as many of them as we can to Hell and damnation with us!"

Six of the Night Riders already lay helplessly on the ground. The remaining horsemen continued firing blindly at the stores. Over the next few minutes three more of the invaders were sent crashing from their mounts as the fire from the unseen townsfolk continued to pour into their ranks.

When there were only three of the riders left on their mounts, a tall, imposing figure wearing the tin star of a marshal came slowly out of the saloon, shouting to the townsfolk to hold their fire. Slowly the noise died away and an eerie silence hung like a stifling pall over the street. Only the crackling of the flames could be heard.

"It's finished!" called the man with the star in the sudden hush to the wounded survivors among the Night Riders crowded close together on their bucking horses in the centre of the street. "You ain't got a chance. Throw down your guns."

The leader of the Night Riders, bleeding from half a dozen wounds, swayed in his saddle and glared down at the marshal.

"Tod Washburn!" he snarled. "I should have guessed it was you. Nobody else in this one-horse town would have had the guts to stand up to us. How did you manage to stuff some starch into this lot, Marshal? Must have taken a lot of doing."

"I told you to throw down your gun," said the marshal. "You're as good as dead, Clem Harkness."

"So are you, Washburn, ever think of that?" snarled the leader of the Night Riders, and aimed his heavy Colt at the lawman and fired.

The bullet from his massive revolver

sent the marshal spinning back against a hitching post. He dropped his Colt. At the sight of the incapacitated lawman the townsfolk concealed in the buildings hesitated.

"What are we going to do?" whispered a terrified Ellcott, on the saloon roof. "If Washburn is dead, we ain't got a chance."

"I'm getting the hell away from here," said Kennedy urgently, throwing away his rifle and darting for the trap-door in the roof.

Down on the street Harkness levelled his Colt for the second time in the deadly silence which had fallen.

"What did I tell you?" he sneered. "They ain't got the heart for a fight without you to lead em, Tod."

Washburn returned his gaze, with sombre eyes which refused to beg. A solitary shot rang out, thudding into the body of the leader of the Night Riders. A momentary look of surprise clouded Harkness's eyes. For a moment the leader of the invaders tried to look for his unseen assailant. Then he slumped lifeless from his saddle. The townsfolk hidden in the houses seemed to come to life again at the sight of the dead leader on the ground. They took their cue from the unexpected and lethal shot and poured round after round into the surviving riders, until the ground was littered with dead and dying men and kicking horses.

Holding his bleeding shoulder Marshal Washburn staggered forward. He made sure that there was no life left in the riders on the ground. Then he walked unsteadily down the street, his eyes searching the darkness in the direction of the shot which had saved his life. When he saw what had occurred his eyes widened in amazement.

"John Prayer!" he demanded in scandalized tones. "What in tarnation are you doing out on the street tonight of all nights?"

The ten-year old boy lay on his stomach where he had dived to pick up the Colt discarded by one of the dying Night Riders. He spat the dust from his mouth and stared wordlessly at the body of the Night Rider leader he had just killed with one lucky shot from the weapon he had picked up with both hands and fired in a single movement. Washburn ran forward and picked the boy up.

"Are you all right?" he asked distractedly, his hands searching the boy for signs of wounds.

"I'm fine, sir," replied the boy dazedly. "I got him, didn't I?"

"You got him all right," said the lawman grimly. "Saved my life as well, when nobody else had the guts to take the drop on him. You just picked up a gun from the dust and brought Clem Harkness down with a single shot in the dark. Never seen anything like it. I ain't never going to forget it, son, nor is anyone else in the town. But what am I going to tell Mrs Washburn when she hears that you were out here?"

The boy looked at the lawman

appealingly. "Maybe we could both lie a little, Marshal?" he hazarded hopefully.

In spite of himself Tod Washburn laughed. It was not something he did often. He released the boy. As he did so his foot came into contact with something on the ground. He stooped and wonderingly picked up the Night Riders' flag. It was festooned with bullet holes and had been shot away entirely from its supporting pole. Washburn folded the square of cloth and handed it to the gaping boy.

"Here," he said gruffly. "Reckon you've done as much to earn this as anybody. Now get back home, do you hear me? I've got a mess of work to finish up here."

"Yes sir," said John Prayer, clutching the tattered flag closely to his chest.

Hero-worship illuminating his eyes he watched the town marshal walk slowly back to the bodies of the Night Riders and start giving concise orders to the now subdued townsfolk emerging from the buildings on both sides of the main street.

John Prayer turned to walk back home. He knew that Mrs Washburn would be waiting for him, half out of her mind with worry at what might have happened to her husband. Her mood would not be considerably improved when she discovered that her adopted son had also been embroiled in the gun fight.

The boy stopped suddenly. He was still close to the boarding house. He hesitated for a few moments, wondering whether he had enough courage to do the second extraordinary thing that he had a mind to do on that most eventful and unusual night. The second matter would be harder, because he had picked up and fired the Colt in the heat of the moment, spurred on by a desire to save the life of the man who meant the most in the world to him.

What he was going to do now he would have to do cold and that was a far harder proposition.

Nevertheless with great trepidation he climbed on to the verandah of the boarding house and went inside the building. A pretty woman in a black dress was standing in the dining room, clutching a sobbing girl to her side. The girl was about eight or nine and had the same auburn hair and attractive features as the woman who was holding her. The woman looked surprised when she saw the boy.

"John Prayer," she said in mingled anger and astonishment. "What are you doing out on a night like this?"

"It's all right, Mrs Richmond," said the boy reassuringly. "It's all over now. You can tell Kate to stop crying." He paused and then awkwardly held out the tattered and crumpled flag in his hands towards the girl. The girl ceased sobbing and held the flag in solemn astonishment.

"Thought you might like this, Kate," John Prayer told her. "Sort of a keepsake like."

The girl kneaded the piece of cloth in her hands, saying nothing. John Prayer's nerve suddenly failed him and he turned and ran back out into the night.

2

THE two drunken saddle-bums were making a fair to middling job of breaking up the saloon this early in the morning. So far they had smashed the piano and wrecked three tables. Any minute now, judged Prayer, they would be starting in on the ornate mirror behind the bar. It had been brought six hundred miles overland from Kansas City and was the pride and joy of Pa Kennedy's cold and miserly heart. He paid more heed to that ornament than he did to any of his kith and kin.

Prayer stood quietly in the doorway, choosing his moment to act. He remembered what Marshal Washburn had told him. Choose your moment, the old man had said, always choose your moment; for a lawman accurate timing is sometimes the only thing standing between you and a slow and nasty death. On this occasion if he moved too soon the tramps would feel aggrieved and put up a fight. On the other hand, if he left it too late the mirror would be destroyed and a vindictive Pa Kennedy would insist on the saddle-tramps being thrown into gaol, where they would have to be fed and would generally disrupt his life as marshal of Trail's End. He had been appointed only a month ago, upon Marshal Washburn's death, and he was finding the job hard enough without wet-nursing any saddle-tramps.

As he looked on Prayer figured that one more table would probably just about do it. Almost on cue, laughing drunkenly the tramps overturned the piece of fragile furniture with a splintering of rotten wood, and lurched menacingly towards the bar. Prayer eased his way into the room, tall and lathe-thin, with already a hint of the considerable heft that would soon develop in his chest and shoulders, and cat-light on his feet. The dusty, unkempt saloon was empty except for the two vagrants.

"Reckon that's enough, boys," drawled Prayer. He tried to keep his voice casual but firm as Washburn had taught him. "You've had your fun."

The men turned in surprise. Only one of the men carried a gun but both of them were big, and odds of two to one were never healthy. Both tramps were dressed in cheap trail clothes, still covered in dust from long days and nights sleeping rough on the trail.

"Who the hell are you, kid?" snarled the tramp with the gun. He was tall and angular, with a big nose and eyes that twitched restlessly. A faded knife-scar ran down one cheek.

Prayer moved out of the shadows in to a patch of sunlight flooding through the window. He was careful to keep the sun at his back. His eyes flickered down to the tin star pinned on his shirt front and then back to the two vagrants.

"Lawman!" sneered the saddle-tramp.

He spat contemptuously on the floor. "They taking them from the cradle these days?"

"Get back on your horses and ride peaceful out of town," said Prayer evenly. These men were dangerous nuisances, but not men to be greatly feared. He would have to learn to deal with trouble-makers like these in his sleep if he was to have a long life as a marshal. "I won't even ask you to pay for the damage."

"Who's going to make us?" asked the tall man truculently.

"I don't want any trouble," Prayer told him, not raising his voice from its level monotone. "You've probably spent your last few cents on Pa Kennedy's rotgut red-eye, which is why you're feeling a mite frisky now. If I was to arrest you you'd never be able to meet your fine, and the town would have to pay for your keep while you were in gaol. Better for everybody if you ride on."

"Reckon you could take us?"

demanded the tall saddle-tramp, his voice rising to a shriek and his anger as quick and obvious as a flash-storm. "I'd like to see that." He moved menacingly towards Prayer until the marshal could smell the stench of his breath.

"That's far enough," said Prayer.

"I've seen you before," said the other saddle-tramp, speaking for the first time. He was older and shorter than his companion, but broader across the shoulders, nervy but not nearly as drunk. Automatically Prayer pegged him as the jackal living off the scraps provided by the muscle of the younger tramp. He was staring hard at the marshal through thoughtful, shifty eyes.

"Last time we rode through you was the deputy" he said slowly, working things out carefully in his mind. "The marshal was an old guy. What happened to him?"

"He died," said Prayer. It still hurt him to say the words. "Heart attack."

The smaller man grinned craftily. "And the town council saved a few bucks by giving the badge to a kid, huh?" he asked. "Big mistake." He glanced at his companion. "Pete, they've left junior in charge of the store!" The tall man scowled and dipped a shoulder. It was a move Washburn had always told Prayer to watch out for. Before the man could complete the movement Prayer had eased his Colt 44 revolver from its holster with the speed of a striking snake. The tall man gaped and allowed his hand to drop harmlessly to his side. There was a short silence.

"Mighty impressive," said the older saddle-tramp slowly after a time. "So you're fast on the draw. So what? There's a mess of difference between drawing and shooting."

"I can shoot too," said Prayer, not taking his eyes off the tall man. "You're welcome to try me."

The smaller tramp sighed regretfully and shook his head, as if coming to an unpleasant decision. "Not this time," he said. "Come on, Pete. We're going."

His companion hesitated. "He wouldn't shoot," he said, plainly trying to convince himself. "Not a kid marshal of a hick town."

"Maybe he would, maybe he wouldn't," said the other man flatly. "I'd hate to live off the difference. Try him if you've a mind to. Me, I'm riding on."

Pete moved from one foot to another in his indecision. His eyes reached deep into Prayer's, trying to fathom the marshal's mind. Prayer's gaze did not waver. Then the tall man relaxed and cursed, but there was no heart to it. He turned and lurched out of the saloon after his friend. With studied calm Prayer walked out of the saloon and watched the saddle-tramps unhitch their horses from the rail and climb on to them. He was aware of the racing of his heart but tried to betray no emotion. The smaller man looked down at him. He seemed already to have forgotten their dispute.

"Is it true that Tod Washburn tracked an outlaw for three days and nights across the Indian Territory?" he asked. "They say he tied his wrist to his saddle just in case his horse fell asleep and threw him."

"The story's grown in the telling," said Prayer. "It was only two days and nights. Tod was like that."

The smaller man shook his head admiringly. "You got some mighty big shoes to fill, youngster," he said. "It'll take more than a fast gun, too. Now, we ain't agoing to try you, that's certain sure." His flickering eyes glistened suddenly with unconcealed blood anticipation. "But there are others riding this way who will. We passed Jericho's drive on our way in this morning. Believe me, they're going to tear this town apart when they get here!"

"They'll have to get past me first," said Prayer.

"They'll try," said the older saddle-tramp. "Bet on it. What do they call you, boy?"

"John Prayer."

"I'll listen out for the name," said the older saddle tramp, twisting back in his misshapen saddle. "Seems to me I'm going to be hearing it soon. If you face down Jericho's boys you're either going to end up famous — or dead!"

A malicious grin creased his unshaven face and he spurred his horse away down the main street, followed by the surly and hungover Pete. Without looking round Prayer was aware of the obese Pa Kennedy waddling out of the saloon and standing behind him. The town councillor must have bolted for his room upstairs as soon as the trouble had started. Now that the bother was over he was going to get brave.

"You should have arrested them both," grumbled the saloon proprietor. "That's what we pay you for, son."

"They won't be back," said Prayer indifferently. "I'm going to have more important things to do than wet-nurse a pair of drifters."

"Are you still worried about Jericho?" scoffed Kennedy. "I'm telling you that trail herd coming here is the best thing that ever happened to Trail's End. You'll see."

"Marshal Washburn always said you didn't know what you was talking about," said Prayer, walking away. "Reckon he was right."

"Yeah? Well you're too big for your britches, John Prayer," the incensed saloon owner shouted after him. "You're just a snot-nosed kid! You only got the marshal's job because Tod Washburn spoke up for you on his death-bed, and you was practically kin to the marshal. Hell, this place don't even need a lawman no more. Trail's End is a tamed town!"

Prayer paid no attention to the familiar abuse.

Steadily he walked past the hardware store, the hotel, the livery stable, the Chinese laundry and the hash house, on the way towards the gaol. They were all made of bare board lumber. Paint cost money and there was little of that in the town these days. It was a little past noon but the streets were almost empty. Trail's End was a quiet town. Once, when he had been growing up just before the Civil War, it had been alive twenty-four hours a day. There had been extensive silver workings outside the town and three large spreads within a twenty miles radius. There had even been an army fort on the border of the Indian country to the north-west. Then the ore had run out, droughts had decimated the ranches and the troops had been recalled East. As a result the town had declined to its present moribund state. There was only one hope for its future and that was the newly opened rail-head established two months before when the railroad from Dodge City to the east had finally been laid as far as the town.

Right up to the end Tod Washburn had been convinced that one day the town would regain its former glory.

"Mark my words," he used to say. "Trail's End is too important to wither on the vine. One day something will turn up and this will be a boom town again."

Maybe the old man had been right, thought Prayer; he usually was. At the thought of the former marshal his throat tightened. Everything he had he owed to Washburn, and it was a debt he would never be able to repay. The marshal had rescued him from the streets fourteen years ago as a runt of seven when the wagon train carrying his parents to California had been forced to stop outside the town. An outbreak of scarlet fever had decimated the train and carried off Prayer's parents among the others. By the time some of the surviving pioneers had finished looting the wagon all that was left was a leather trunk containing five blankets, two pillows, a cast-iron frying pan and a family Bible.

Marshal Washburn had rescued the child and the trunk, and he and his wife had taken the frightened boy in and brought him up as their own, giving him the love and care that had transformed him over the years into a self-confident young man. He had always been self-assured, right from the first.

"Always reckon it was lucky you was only seven when that wagon-train robbed you blind," Washburn would chuckle. "Time you was nine you would have lit after 'em like smoke in a storm!"

Mrs Washburn had died three years ago, when Prayer had been eighteen. After they had buried her Washburn had made the youth his deputy. For the last three years he had patiently coached the youth in the craft of the lawman. "One day," he had said gruffly, "you might just be almost as good as I am! In the meantime you'd better just hope I hang on long enough to teach you all you need to know to stay alive."

Well, thought Prayer ruefully, Marshal Washhurn had not lived long enough to turn him into a marshal. He had taught him how to draw and shoot and how to take care of himself in a rough-house brawl, but those were only the surface tricks. The really important things he would now have to learn for himself. He feared it might be a hard process.

He sauntered unhurriedly up the street, politely returning the respectful salutations of the men and women he passed on the way. Without seeming to he took in everything that was happening on the street that morning. The Concord stage-coach was loading up for its weekly trip to Denver to the north-west. The coach could carry nine passengers inside and twelve on top. Today there were only a couple of dispirited-looking drummers in shiny suits with their sample cases boarding the vehicle. Prayer wondered how much longer the company would keep going once the railroad was extended even farther to the west. Things surely were changing, he thought; he only hoped that the changes would be for the best.

Prayer heard the sound of a voice raised in anger. He stopped and located the direction of the altercation and then drifted casually over. The noise was coming from the boardwalk outside the Chinaman's laundry. Deke Kelly, the town drunk, was being castigated by a young cowhand in a dusty shirt and Levis. Prayer did not recognize the irate cowboy. He must be new to the town and he seemed to have a hair-trigger temper. At the moment he was very angry and was shaking the drunk by the front of Deke's filthy shirt. Kelly was making incoherent noises as he tried to free himself.

"All right, boys," said Prayer. "Let's button it all down a mite, shall we?"

The cowhand glared over his shoulder at Prayer. He saw the badge on the other man's chest but did not release his hold on the drunk's shirt-front.

"I'm just teaching this old galoot a lesson," he snarled.

"Reckon Deke is standing in need of all the help he can get," agreed Prayer calmly. "But do you reckon he's in a righteous frame of mind to profit from what you're going to teach him? Maybe if you was to loosen your grip a little it might allow the blood and sense to flow through him easier."

The cowhand looked suspiciously at Prayer and then reluctantly released his grip on the drunk. He was young, a few years older than Prayer, short and squat. His stetson was hanging down his back from its wide strap to reveal a head of ash-blond hair combed forward in a sweeping cowlick. There was an air of arrogance to the cowhand; he looked the sort who did not step aside for anyone.

"Well, Deke," said Prayer easily, "what have you done to upset our visitor."

The old man squinted at the two youngsters in front of him through rheumy, bloodshot eyes. He licked his lips nervously.

"Honest, Marshal, I didn't mean nothing," he whined. "I was just coming up the side of the Chinaman's when I bumped into this young fellow."

"He damn near knocked me off the broadwalk," spat the cowhand.

"Well, mister, I'm sure old Deke didn't mean no harm," said Prayer placatingly. "You can see for yourself he ain't really in no fitting state to know where he's coming from or where he's going to. Why don't you just apologize to the man, Deke, and go about your appointed business?"

"Sure thing, Marshal," gulped the old man eagerly. He turned apologetically to the cowhand. "I'm sorry, youngster, honest. Didn't have no intention of crowding you."

Deke turned and scuttled off, weaving unsteadily along the boardwalk. Prayer turned back to the cowhand. "Deke's all right," he said with a laugh. "I don't think he's been sober for ten years. He comes to rest in some pretty unlikely places, I can tell you."

The cowhand's expression did not

soften. "He should be shot, like a lame horse," he grated. "I'm looking for Pa Kennedy. Where do I find him?"

"Pa's in the saloon," said Prayer slowly, indicating the direction.

The cowhand slouched off without a word. Prayer watched him go and then continued his progress to his office. His mind was working and he was aware of a slight feeling of unease. He was sure that he had seen the quick-tempered young cowhand before, but he could not recollect where.

Mayor Ellcott was waiting for him in his office. Ellcott owned the town provender store. He was a conscientious, worried-looking man in his fifties in a dark grey suit. He stood up as the marshal came in.

"Hello, Jack," said Prayer, dropping into the chair behind his desk. "What are you doing here?"

"Town Council's had a meeting," said Ellcott. "They asked me to see you."

"Town Council's always having

meetings," said Prayer lightly, but he was aware of a tightening in his stomach. There were plenty on the council who thought he was too young and inexperienced for his job.

"This one was special."

"How special?"

"We was talking about Wade Jericho's cattle-drive. Could be the biggest thing ever happened to this town."

Ellcott's eyes flickered around the room like restless flies. Reluctantly he got down to the point. "John, we've got to treat Jericho and his boys with plenty of respect. Council was concerned for me to make that point mighty particular to you. If'n Jericho ain't handled right he could take his next drive to another rail-head. We couldn't stand that. One more bad year and Trail's End could be a ghost town."

"Ain't got no quarrel with Jericho," said Prayer. "Man's a hero. He's just finished one of the longest cattle-drives in history."

"Four hundred miles across some

of the worst country in Kansas," agreed Ellcott enthusiastically. "That man herded more than a thousand longhorns clear across country, just on the chance that they'd make it to Trail's End. And they have, by God! By right Jericho and his wranglers should be a line of doled-out skeletons somewhere along the trail. Instead they're watering their steers a mile outside town. It's a miracle. And it's a miracle that's ended up in our town. Jericho hears a rumour that the railroad has reached us, and he heads out with his cattle on the basis of that say-so. Couple more trips like that and every big rancher from the grasslands in the shadow of the Rockies is going to follow his example along the Jericho Trail. That means we're going to be a big cattle-town, boy. I mean Marshal."

"What's your drift?" asked Prayer. He was aware of what the mayor was going to say next, but he wanted it spelt out.

"I'll tell you my drift. We've got to

persuade Jericho to make a few more cattle-drives along his trail. Just to show that it can be done. Once he's done that the other owners to the north are going to use the trail. And that trail ends here in our town. Railroad will pour money into the stockyards, cowboys will spend their dollars here. Look what happened to Abilene seven or eight years ago. Rail-head turned it into the most prosperous town in the West. That could happen to us. You got any problem with that?"

"Marshal Washburn did."

At the sound of the late marshal's name Ellcott's face shrivelled as if he had been forced to suck on a lemon.

"What about Washburn?" he asked peevishly.

"Soon as he heard that the drive was starting he said that if anyone could do it Wade Jericho was the man."

"So?"

"He also said," went on Prayer quietly, "that Jericho would never do it with ordinary trail-hands. To finish that trail he would need to recruit every hard man in that part of Texas. Men as tough as mountain lions and as heedless as buzzards. Outlaws, renegades, deserters. It would take a special kind of breed to hack out the Jericho Trail."

"Maybe," said Ellcott uncomfortably.

"The sort of man Jericho's brought with him," said Prayer relentlessly. "That sort of man would be stand-up necessary when it came to crossing flooded rivers, fighting off Indians and standing up to bushwhackers, on a diet of jerky and sourdough."

"Goes without saying," muttered the mayor.

"Once the drive was over," went on Prayer, "that same sort of man wouldn't be exactly the sort you'd welcome into a peaceful, law abiding town like Trail's End. That was the way Washburn saw it."

"Tod Washburn's dead," said Mayor Ellcott, trying to laugh but coming out with a dry rattle. "He was a good man in his time, but limited. Only saw straight ahead. We appointed you because we reckoned you'd be more flexible like. Young man like you, with a career to make."

The threat hung in the air like a faint morning mist. Prayer's lips tightened but he ignored the remark.

"You hired me to keep the law in this town," he said.

"And you'll make a good job of it, I'm certain of it," said Ellcott, with sudden forced cheerfulness. The mayor clapped Prayer heartily on the back and consulted his fob watch.

"A little after noon," he announced meaningfully. "School's out! Shouldn't you be out on the street, Marshal? Just in case you should bump into Kate accidental-like?"

In spite of himself Prayer blushed furiously. Ellcott chuckled and headed for the door.

"Only funning," he grinned. "I'll leave you to your courting. In the meantime chew over what the Town

Council wants. Cut plenty of slack for Jericho and his boys should they come into town. Remember now."

The mayor went out. Prayer sat on behind his desk, deep in thought. His eyes flickered round the room. It was small and dark. Off to the right were two cells, with iron-barred doors. Apart from the occasional drunk they had seen no customers for months. The wooden walls of the office were bare except for a few fluttering and tattered Wanted posters. Every day Prayer memorized the faces on those bills. He remembered what had been worrying him out in the street and walked over and consulted the posters carefully. What he saw there made him frown thoughtfully. He took his Colt from its holster and checked the shells.

He looked up at the clock on the wall of his office. Mayor Ellcott had been right. Morning school would be out and Miss Kate would be on her way home from the school where she taught for two hours each morning, to the boarding house she had recently inherited from her mother and which, to the surprise of most townsfolk, she had taken over and was running with great success. He heaved himself to his feet and moved unhurriedly out of the office in to the sunny main street.

Miss Kate was only a few yards away, walking serenely along the boardwalk. She saw the young marshal and stopped. Awkwardly Prayer touched the brim of his stetson.

"Good morning, Marshal," smiled the girl, stopping.

"Miss Kate," gulped Prayer. Desperately he tried to think of something to say. As usual he failed.

The girl smiled encouragingly and did not move. She was about the same age as the marshal, small and pretty, with brown eyes and a small turned-up nose. Her mother had sent her to college in Kansas City to be trained as a teacher, but a month earlier, upon the sudden death of her mother,

Kate had returned to Trail's End and showed every sign of settling down there, teaching in the morning and spending the rest of the day running the boarding house. As children the two of them had played together, but ever since Kate had returned from the city, a sophisticated young lady, Prayer had hardly dared to pluck up the courage to talk to her.

"Will you be at the church social on Saturday night?" she asked innocently.

It took a few seconds for it to register with Prayer that there was a whisper of an invitation in the girl's words. When it did he half-way to strangled himself getting his answer out.

"Surely will," he nodded eagerly.

"Perhaps I'll see you there, Marshal John Prayer," said Kate pertly, and continued on her way towards the boarding house without a backward glance.

Prayer watched her go, hardly daring to believe that the girl had been so forward in her hinting. A warm glow began to spread inside him. With an ache to his heart he wished that the social was not the best part of a week away.

"Marshal Prayer!"

Prayer turned in the direction of the shout. Mayor Ellcott and Pa Kennedy, the saloon owner, were hurrying towards him. With them was a third man, leading a horse by its bridle. The newcomer was the cowhand who had had the run-in with Deke Kelly outside the livery stable. He scowled when he saw the marshal. Prayer noticed how deeply the clothes of the young cowhand were ingrained with the dust of long riding and hard sleeping. The man wore his gunbelt low-slung.

"Marshal, this here is Brett Henry," said Mayor Ellcott eagerly. "He's one of Wade Jericho's drive-crew. Mr Jericho sent him ahead to fix the details of him and his boys watering his herd outside the town on the open range until the cattle trucks get here."

"Howdy," nodded Prayer. "Brett Henry, you say?"

"That's right," said the trail-hand briefly, throwing the reins of his mount round the hitching post outside the marshal's office. His eyes flickered over Prayer, noting the stillness of the young law officer.

"You got a problem with that, Marshal?" he asked insolently.

"I might have," said Prayer, not backing up to allow the other into the office. The two young men stood, eye to eye, on the dusty street in the noon sun.

"Come on boys, what is this?" asked Ellcott, trying to laugh the situation off. "Let's go inside and sort the details out."

"What's your beef?" asked Henry softly.

"Matter of identity," said Prayer. "You tell me you're called Brett Henry. I fancy that's stretching the truth a mite. Your face is on one of the bills on my wall. Only there you're called

43

Mike Clegg, and you're wanted for murder."

The trail-hand's expression did not change, but he took a smooth, practised step backwards. Pa Kennedy lumbered appealingly towards Prayer.

"Come on, son," he wheezed. "Whatever this man's done, it wasn't in Trail's End, was it?"

"Texas," said Prayer.

Kennedy spread his large, flipper-like hands. "There you are then," he said. "Ain't none of our never-mind. He's one of Wade Jericho's men, and Wade's going to bring prosperity to this town. Let it ride, son. What happened in Texas is all washed down the river."

"That's right, we'll all go inside and have a drink. I'm sure you've got a bottle somewhere, Marshal," said Ellcott quickly, with his customary meaningless laugh.

Prayer ignored the two town councillors. All his attention was on the trail-herder standing coiled menacingly in front of

44

him. The marshal extended a hand.

"I'll take your gun-belt, Mike," he said quietly.

The trail-hand shook his head. "Like hell you will, boy," he sneered.

"I don't want you making no mistake about this," warned Prayer. "I'm arresting you for murder."

A guffaw rattled in the other man's throat, so brief it could have been a cough. Suddenly his hand swooped contemptuously for his holster. Then he made his mistake. In order to impress the onlookers he used the Border Fan, sweeping back the hammer of his heavy Smith and Wesson with the heel of his free hand. It was a showy gesture but it threw the gun-fighter briefly off balance and it added a fraction of a second to the timing of his draw. In that period Prayer freed his Colt smoothly from its holster and fired the six-shooter twice.

The bullets slammed into the body of the trail-hand, sending him staggering backwards. He twisted round and fell face first into the dust, where he lay without moving.

Mayor Ellcott was the first to reach the body. He knelt by the side of the trail hand and conducted a brief inspection. Then he looked up accusingly at Prayer.

"He's dead!" he said harshly. "Marshal, you've just signed this town's death-warrant with your six-shooter!"

3

THE beans on Wade Jericho's plate were too hot for his taste, so he placed the plate by his side. There was plenty of time, he decided. Calmly he looked round at the trail-hands scattered around the camp-site, eating the food prepared by the cook at the side of his chuck-wagon. Only Gradey, the half-breed cook, son of a Sioux mother and an Irish prospector, hawk-nosed, grey haired and solitary, sat apart from the others. Without appearing to he was keeping a watchful eye on the trail-boss, ready to come to Jericho's assistance if one of the trail-hands started anything.

It was a luxury to be able to eat at his ease in this fashion, thought Jericho, even if the atmosphere was strained. For the last two months meals had been snatched affairs, often eaten in the saddle as the frightened and mutinous longhorns were urged along the hazardous trails, up the sides of hills and across flooded rivers. Now for a couple of days until the cattle-trucks arrived it should be possible to relax.

Jericho frowned at the thought and faced up to the problem which had been haunting him ever since they had pitched camp. Too much spare time might not be a good thing for the type of cowhand he had brought along with him. He had taken a great deal of care over their selection. Each man had to be tough, self-reliant and ruthless, all traits needful in riders charged with moving more than a thousand steers hundreds of miles across uncharted and almost impassable country.

The one thing he had been careful not to do was to ask any of his cowhands about his past. Some he had recognized by reputation as gunslingers and outlaws wanted by the law in a dozen territories, even if they had given him false names. Others he had never heard of, but he could tell from their wary bearing and their vicious conduct on the trail that they had been schooled in rough territory. Some of them were probably glad to be clear of pursuing lawmen for the period of the drive; others had been attracted by the generous bonus he had been offering and the challenge presented by the proposed journey.

Well, somehow they had done it, thought Jericho. They had covered four hundred miles, losing only thirty steers and not a single rider. The trail-hands had earned a good time in the local town, that was for sure. He only hoped that the good time would be restricted to a few fights and a comparatively few breakages.

"What's the town like, Mr Jericho?" asked one of the younger hands, looking across and breaking in on his train of thought.

"Trail's End?" asked Jericho, giving

the matter some consideration. "One-horse place. Only after the last eight weeks it'll look like paradise to you. Rowdy it ain't. Main thing ever happened there was when they shot down the Night Riders in '60, just before the War."

"Trail's End was a Yankee town wasn't it?" asked another of the hands disapprovingly.

Jericho nodded. "Kansas was split in half back then," he said. "Some were for the Union, some were for the Confederacy. They used to raid one another long before the real war started. Union supporters called themselves the Night Riders, because they would attack the pro-slave towns at night. Only the night they decided to raid Trail's End somebody gave them away. People in the town were waiting for them, armed and ready. Killed every one of the Night Riders in the main street. Shot 'em down from ambush."

"Sort of low-down trick you'd expect from Yankees," said a trail-hand bitterly.

Most of the others nodded agreement. Jericho knew that the majority of the hands with him must have fought for the Union during the war, and those that had not were keeping their mouths shut on this occasion.

"Happened on both sides," he said. "Bloody Bill Anderson and his boys took the rebel yell into a fair few Union towns as well. Evened itself out, I reckon."

"Anyway, when are we going into town?" demanded one of the trail-herders abruptly.

"I sent Brett ahead to fix things up," said Jericho, not looking across at the herder, a tall, spidery man called Kilcannon. He had already marked Kilcannon down as a loud-mouth and a potential trouble-maker and he had been expecting some show of defiance from him now that the long ride was over. In a way he rather hoped that the other man would start something and allow him to stamp his authority on the bunch.

"What's to fix?" demanded Kilcannon brusquely.

"How much money you got?" asked Jericho.

"Nothing; you know that," said the tall trail-herder truculently. "Reckon you'd be fixing to pay us now the trip's over."

There were cautious murmurs of agreement from the other hands as they cast surreptitious glances across the site to see how the trail-boss was reacting to Kilcannon's hostility. No one was prepared to face the notoriously hot-tempered rancher but they were all happy for Kilcannon to test the temperature of the water. At the moment Jericho's face betrayed no emotion.

"I don't have any more money with me than you do," he said.

Kilcannon began to edge across the area. Still Jericho did not move.

"However," Jericho went on evenly, "I've telegraphed Chicago, and buyers from the stock companies are on their way here now in a special cattle train to bid for the herd. Should be here in a couple of days with the money. When they arrive you'll get paid off — with your bonus."

Kilcannon was closer to him now, arrogance stretched tautly across his face. The cowhand loosened his shoulders in a series of cat-like ripples as he approached.

"Furthermore," added Jericho as if he had not noticed the other man's advance, "I've sent Brett ahead into Trail's End with a message. I've told him to tell the storekeepers there that each of you is good for ten dollars in the town today and tomorrow, and that I'll stand surety for you for that much if you spend it when you get there."

"Well, that's a little better," said Kilcannon, mollified to a certain extent. "Why didn't you say so before? Come on, boys, let's ride into town and spend some of Mr Jericho's money."

"Not so fast," said Jericho. "We'll wait for Brett to get back first. Then

I'll send half of you in to town, while the rest look after the steers."

Kilcannon spat. "If you think I'm going to spend any more time on those longhorns, forget it," he said with feeling. "I've been eating their dust for too long. I'm riding into town now."

"Not until I say so," said Jericho mildly. Kilcannon took a menacing step forward, until he was standing directly over the trail-boss.

"We ain't on the trail now," he said flatly. "You've got no more control, Jericho."

Jericho sighed gently. "Is that a fact?" he enquired.

On the other side of the camp site he saw Gradey put down his plate and stand up, ready to move over to his side. Jericho shook his head slightly. Gradey sat down again but maintained a watchful posture. Jericho stood up in one fluent movement. As he did so he picked up with his left hand the plate of beans at his side. He rammed the plate of hot beans hard into the face of the cowhand. Kilcannon screamed with pain and automatically raised his hands to claw away the beans running down his face. Jericho hit him in the stomach with a jolting right and then spun round to the trail herder's side and swung a looping left into Kilcannon's kidneys.

The thin man groaned and began to sag to the ground. Jericho helped him on his way with a vicious kick to the kneecap. As Kilcannon sprawled on the ground like a puppet whose strings had been severed, the trail boss drew back his foot and kicked him several more times in the ribs. Kilcannon twitched violently and then lay still.

Jericho's eyes travelled enquiringly over the camp site. Some of the trail hands were looking faintly alarmed, while the tougher among the others were grinning appreciatively at the comprehensive manner in which Jericho had dealt with the rebellion, and were looking speculatively at the trail-boss as they decided that any time to face down Wade Jericho definitely had not yet arrived.

"I say we wait for Brett to get back," said Jericho. "Anybody got any objections?"

From the lack of response around the camp fire it was plain that nobody had any objections. Jericho nodded and picked up his plate. Taking his time he walked slowly across the site to the chuck-wagon, his attitude defying anyone to stop him. No one moved. Kilcannon was left to groan unheeded and untended on the ground.

Jericho walked round to the far side of the wagon and helped himself to some more beans from the cook-pot simmering over the fire. Gradey stood up and sidled round to meet him. There was a hint of a smile on the half-breed's thin lips.

"What are you grinning at?" demanded Jericho sourly, shovelling some beans on to his plate.

"You're losing your touch," Gradey

told him lightly. "I can remember when the first two punches would have been enough. Now you've got to kick 'em half to death as well."

"The punches were enough then," growled Jericho. "The kicking was just for show."

He pushed some of the beans absently into his mouth. Gradey waited patiently. He had ridden with the other man long enough to know when Jericho was doing some serious thinking.

"Did you ever meet such an ordinary bunch?" demanded Jericho abruptly. "Backstabbers and general low-life every man."

"We've met their equal," murmured Gradey. "Time we caught up with some of Bill Quantrill's boys after their raid on Lawrence; they was pretty low to the ground. Them that was left alive."

"At least there was a war then," grumbled Jericho. "These sidewinders here are low down just for the sheer hell of it."

"You said you didn't want no Sunday school teachers when you hired 'em," Gradey reminded the trail-boss.

"I know what I said," replied Jericho, still inwardly fuming.

"Reckon you know they're going to turn on you like snakes any day now, as well," said Gradey, undisturbed.

"Not yet they ain't" said the other man, finishing his beans and dropping his knife and plate.

"When then?" asked the half-breed.

"When they think they can rob me as well as kill me," said Jericho, walking away. "Make it a lot more interesting for 'em."

Gradey watched the big man walk back across the site, ignoring the disgruntled trail-herders. Jericho walked as if he owned the ground he walked over. But he had always done that, even when he had been half-starving as a bounty-hunter when Gradey had first met him more than twenty years ago. Wade Jericho was a proud and dangerous man, thought the half-breed. Whatever the trail-herders were plotting to do to him, he would bet that the trail-boss had laid his own plans to pay them back in spades.

4

JOHN PRAYER looked down at the lifeless body of the trail-hand. The young marshal's throat was dry and his hands were trembling. This was the first man he had ever killed in a gunfight. With an effort he put his Colt back in its holster. It took him several attempts. He was dimly aware of a crowd gathering. He looked down to the far end of the street. At the sounds of the shots Kate had turned and was gazing in horror at the body on the ground. Her eyes travelled upwards and for a moment they met Prayer's. Then the girl turned and half-ran down the street towards the boarding house, her hand at her throat.

"Just what in hell have you done?" demanded an outraged Pa Kennedy. "That's Wade Jericho's man you've gunned down."

"He was a wanted man. He drew first," grunted Prayer, determined not to display his feelings of shock and revulsion to the onlookers.

Mayor Ellcott stood up from his examination of the corpse. He was quivering with fear and rage.

"Marshal Prayer, you hold the law too rigid in your hand!" he choked. "You could have posted that man out of the town. There was no need to kill him."

"What will Jericho do when he finds out that we've shot his rider?" asked Kennedy in stunned tones.

"Only one way to find out," said Prayer, moving forward. He scrutinized the fast-increasing crowd and picked out two of the biggest men on its fringes.

"You two load the cowboy on to his horse," he ordered. "I'll take him out to Jericho and explain what happened."

"Don't be a damned fool!" snapped Pa Kennedy. "You go out there to Jericho and his sidewinders with that body and they'll cut you down like tall grass."

"Would you rather Jericho and his men found out when they come into town?" asked Prayer curtly.

"God, no!" burst out Ellcott. "They'll like to burn the place down. Best you rode out, Marshal Prayer."

"I thought you might see it my way," said Prayer drily.

The body of the dead trail-driver was slumped on its stomach across the saddle of his horse, with his legs trailing on one side and his head and torso on the other. At first his horse shied, sensing the presence of death and unwilling to bear the inert body of its former owner, but eventually it settled and stood trembling and sweating. Prayer unhitched his own horse from the tie-rail and eased himself into the saddle. One of the bystanders unhitched the dead cowboy's horse and handed the reins to the marshal. Prayer turned both horses, scattering the crowd, and began to walk both mounts down the main street. As he went he could hear the noise of the crowd spreading like an avalanche behind him.

He did not look to left or right as he transported his grisly cargo down the long street and out of the small town. His heart was beating hard, not from the effects of the gun-fight but at the knowledge of what he was riding into. He tried to recall what he had heard of Wade Jericho and wondered how to separate the fact from the legend. The man had been a hero in the War, fighting for the Union at Bull Run and Gettysburg, and afterwards had served as a hired gun in some of the bloodiest range-wars on the Kansas-Missouri border. There were long unexplained gaps in the man's life, and it was these periods that fuelled some of the more bizarre stories about him. There seemed pretty conclusive evidence at least that he had ridden shotgun for the Wells Fargo line and served as a bounty-hunter for the Pinkerton Agency for a while, before putting together enough of a poke to buy his own spread and build it over the last five years into one of the biggest cattle ranches in neighbouring Colorado. It was rumoured that Wade Jericho carried eight major wounds on his body, and that did not count the lance and arrow cuts he had received from the Sioux on his forays into the Badlands of South Dakota.

If only half of what they said about the rancher was true he was the last man to be told that one of his hired hands was dead, thought Prayer grimly. Automatically he felt for the handle of his new Winchester 73 in its scabbard. Hell, he thought wryly, releasing his grip, I don't need guns; strong and urgent prayer is the only thing likely to keep me alive past sundown.

He rode past the boarding house and restaurant once run by Kate's mother. All the patrons were out on the street, gawking at him as he rode by. Prayer saw Kate in the background. She was wearing a gingham pinafore over her dress. The girl was looking with concern at him. Prayer touched the brim of his hat with a finger. Kate raised a hand in farewell. She looked troubled.

When at last he was free of the last wooden shacks of Trail's End Prayer increased his pace, jerking on the reins of the dead cowboy's horse to make it keep pace with his own pinto. He skirted the cedar forest and rode past the old silver-mine workings. Then he moved steadily across the long meadow grass watered by the creeks of the Clear River, a tributary of the broad and winding Arkansas waterway. The sun was still loafing unhurriedly overhead, while a brisk breeze skimmed across the plains.

Prayer smelt the cattle even before he could hear them. There were over a thousand head according to the rumours, and even spread out over the grazing land as they would be now, there were enough of them to perfume the air with their particular stench.

As he grew closer to the big bend of the Clear the marshal saw the first of the herd. Rumour had been right. There were well over a thousand head scattered over the lush grazing land in the wide curve of the river. The longhorns were all colours, cream, black, brown, yellow and all the combinations in between as they fed contentedly after their long drive. A couple of trail-herders were riding watchfully on the fringes of the scattered herd. The rest of the drivers were gathered about the chuck-wagon, collecting their midday meal from the half breed cook officiating busily at the pots swinging over several wood fires.

Prayer wondered how much money on the hoof he was looking at. Longhorns could be bought for three dollars a head on the open range. When they reached the rail-heads buyers from the East were prepared to pay between thirty and forty dollars each for them. Wade Jericho was already reputed to be a wealthy man. After this drive there would be no doubt about it.

As he drew closer Prayer noticed the bed rolls stored under the trees of a small copse growing down to the water's edge. Farther along there was a small hill. Someone had hacked a dug-out into the side of the mound. A skin of rawhide served as a makeshift door across the entrance.

The cowboys saw him while he was still half a mile away. They recognized the horse accompanying the marshal's mount, and its slumped burden. Silently they put down their tin plates and mugs and fanned out ominously as Prayer approached. The marshal saw without surprise that each trail-herder carried a gunbelt.

Prayer fought back the urge to turn his horse and ride hell-for-leather back to the town. He rode on, stiff backed and tall in the saddle, until he was facing the group of trail-hands close up. They were a lean, craggy, flint-faced lot, their skins burnt brown by weeks of exposure to the sun and wind.

They stood with the casual confidence of men who had faced down most troubles known to man and nature. Only riders of real ability and courage could have carved out the Jericho Trail in the way they had.

A stocky man with piercing black eyes and a mouth so thin it could have been shaped by a knife thrust his way forward. His gaze flickered over the body on the horse at Prayer's side.

"What's this?" he demanded harshly.

"I'm John Prayer, Marshal of Trail's End," said the youth. "I tried to arrest this man, but he made a fight of it."

A collective sullen growl went up from the throats of the assembled cowhands. They began to edge forward like a pack of menacing wolves. Prayer's horse shied nervously. The marshal fought to control the spirited animal.

"Get him off his mount," ordered the stocky man.

Prayer reached for his holster. He heard the immediate rattle of bolts. In a moment he was staring down the barrels of half a dozen Sharps carbines. Prayer stayed his hand and expressionlessly returned it to the pommel of his saddle. A wedge of cowhands surged forward and reached his sweating mount. Their calloused hands reached up to drag the marshal down.

"Hold it!"

The command echoed like a rifle-shot across the camp-site. The trail-herders stopped and stepped back reluctantly. Prayer looked across at the dug-out in the side of the hill. A man had ripped back the rawhide covering and had stepped out of the makeshift dwelling. Prayer knew that this had to be Wade Jericho, friend and drinking companion of such notables as Buffalo Bill Cody and sworn enemy to others, like Wild Bill Hickock. The man was about the same height as the marshal, over six feet, but thirty pounds heavier, all of it extra sinewy muscle on the arms and upper body of a man in the peak of condition. He was a year or two either side of forty, with a drooping black moustache below a nose which had been broken more than once. He was dressed like the other trail-herders in store-bought shirt and vest, hardwearing Levi pants, a wide-brimmed stetson. It was his eyes which made him stand out. They were brown, piercing and proud, the eyes of a man who would command any situation he found himself in. Those eyes took in the dead body slung over the back of the horse, and the tin star on the chest of the young lawman.

"What happened to Brett?" he asked quietly, not moving across the intervening distance.

"This kid claims to have gunned him down," replied the stocky man angrily.

"That right?" asked Jericho.

Prayer nodded. "He was wanted for murder," he told the trail boss. "When I tried to take him in he drew on me. I didn't have any option."

Unhurriedly Jericho walked across to the group of men confronting the marshal. His eyes took in the straight-backed young rider towering over the men on foot. The rancher's eyes strayed to the star on Prayer's chest.

"Sounds like you take that badge kind of serious," he commented.

"I do," replied the marshal.

"It don't mean nothing out here," burst out the stocky man vindictively. "This territory's out of your jurisdiction. County sheriff is the law out here. You've only got the say-so in Trail's End."

"He knows that," said Jericho impatiently. "He didn't have to come out on to the range. He chose to do it." He raised his shrewd eyes to the marshal again. "Just what are you doing here?" he asked.

"Wanted to let you know what I'd done," said Prayer stiffly. "I'm not sorry for it, and I'd do the same again. But I don't want trouble with you and your hands unless I'm forced into it."

"That's mighty considerate of you," said Wade Jericho softly. "Just what

71

sort of trouble do you think you might be able to give a dozen guns?"

Prayer shrugged. "We won't know until the time comes," he said.

Jericho held the marshal's gaze for a long time. Then he turned to the others.

"Get Brett down off his horse," he commanded. "I'll ride into town later and fix up his burial for tomorrow."

"Is that all you're going to do about it?" shouted the stocky man. "Brett rode with us from the beginning."

"He was a hot-head," said Jericho indifferently. "I sent him into town on an errand and he got in above his head with the marshal. That's all there is to it, Leif. It's over. Let it lie."

At the mention of the stocky man's name Prayer felt a sudden stir of interest and apprehension.

"Leif?" he asked. "Are you Billy Leif from Wyoming?"

The stocky man stared up at him, hatred blazing in his eyes. "What about it?" he asked.

"Your name's on a poster too," said the young marshal calmly. "Murder and armed robbery in three states. There's paper out on you."

In a few seconds the group of trail herders had scattered for cover in all directions as Leif backed off a few paces, his face flushed with rage, his lips drawn back in a sneer and his hand hovering over his holster.

"You aiming to take me in, Marshal?" he asked thickly. "'Cause better lawmen than you have tried and failed in that particular."

"If I have to," said Prayer.

He kept his eyes fixed on the outlaw's face and wondered if he had come to the end of his trail. Even if he could outdraw such an experienced gun-fighter as Leif, which was unlikely, the other trail herders would shoot him before he could even turn his horse. Well, maybe he could put up a show and not disgrace himself as the others gunned him down, he thought wryly.

"That's enough!" said Wade Jericho

with authority. The trail boss stared coldly up at Prayer.

"Son, you've said yourself you've got no authority out here," he said. "Turn your horse and head back for Trail's End, while you've still got the chance."

"The hell he will," snarled Billy Leif, still half-crouched in the traditional gun-fighter's deadly pose.

Jericho swung round unhurriedly to face the outlaw. "As for you, Leif," he said, "you know my rules. Any man who pulls a gun to kill somebody except raiders or Indians on my cattle-drive, I'll hang from the nearest tree."

The rancher waited patiently for Leif to reply. The outlaw's furtive gaze sped from face to face in the group about him, his hand was still cocked uncertainly over his holster.

"Are you going to let this kid get away with killing Brett?" he yelped furiously.

"I'll deal with that in my own way in my own time," answered Jericho.

"In the meantime back-up, or it'll be personal between you and me, Billy."

The warning fell to the ground and lay there as if encased in steel. The other cowhands looked apprehensively on. Slowly, as if the action was causing him considerable pain, Leif came out of his crouch and allowed his gun hand to dangle harmlessly at his side. He swore luridly and walked away towards the chuckwagon, holstering his revolver unwillingly. Thoughtfully Jericho watched him go. Then the rancher turned to Prayer. His face was schooled to reveal no emotion but Prayer thought he saw a fleeting glint of respect in the older man's eyes.

"You've got sand riding out here, kid," he said briefly. "But I don't give much for your common-sense. Don't let that star on your chest go to your head. There's half a dozen men in this outfit who could out-draw, out-ride and out-fight you on the best day you ever saw. Now get out of here while you've still got the chance."

"Yes, Mr Jericho," said Prayer respectfully. "There's just one more thing I'd like to say to your hands, begging your pardon." The marshal looked steadily across at the resentful cowhands facing him. "You're all welcome in Trail's End, as long as you behave yourselves," he said clearly. "That is unless any one of you is posted. If there's a notice on you and I find it, then that man will be arrested if he attempts to enter the town. I hope that's plain enough for you."

He wheeled his horse about, ignoring the mutinous chorus of complaints coming from the assembled trail-drivers. Without looking back he cantered his mount across the grasslands by the side of the river. As Prayer rode his mind was busy with what he had seen and heard at the camp. He had finally met Wade Jericho and that was an event in itself, like meeting a living part of the history of the West. The man was every bit as powerful as men had said, not so much from what he had said or done, but simply for what he was.

He had also encountered Jericho's trail-drivers. Prayer frowned at the thought. They were just as tough as their boss but without the rancher's sense of justice. They were also a whole lot meaner. He had only recognized Brett Henry and Billy Leif from their likenesses on the Wanted posters but he would bet that every one of the rugged trail hands was being sought by the law somewhere. It was a problem he would have to face if the cowhands ever came into town.

His horse was tired from the long ride out to the trail camp, so Prayer took his time riding back to town. He guided his mount along the contours of the river bank, stopping every so often to allow it to drink and graze, instead of riding directly across country.

It was not until he was almost back at the old silver works that the first shots were directed at him.

The abandoned mine consisted of a number of tunnels, supported by decaying timbers, driven through the side of a hill a few hundred yards from the broad stretch of river. Piles of boulders blasted from the hill lay in large piles across the ground, from the mine shaft down to the water. Prayer's horse was picking its way carefully through the mounds of rubble when the brisk reports of rifle shots echoed among the stones and sent puffs of dust rising from the ground ahead of him.

Prayer rolled out of the saddle on to the ground, wrestling his Winchester from its scabbard as he did so. The frightened horse whinnied and galloped away. The scattered piles of stones which had given the bushwhackers their hiding place also served to protect the marshal as he dived across the intervening ground and came to a halt behind a heap of boulders.

There was a brief pause as the ambushers tried to locate him and then more cracks as the bullets buried themselves in the ground a few yards to the marshal's left. By this time

Prayer had worked out that the shots were coming from behind a pile of rocks immediately in front of the boarded-up main shaft of the old mine. Prayer judged that there were no more than three of them sheltering behind the boulders. There was enough open ground to his left and right to make it unlikely that they would be able to outflank him. On the other hand the open land on either side and broad, low-banked river behind him meant that he was effectively pinned down for as long as the bushwhackers wanted to shoot at him.

More shots spat from the mine shaft across the intervening space. They were random and haphazard, so Prayer knew that the three men had not worked out precisely where he was. He resisted the temptation to fire back. To do so would serve little useful purpose and would only give his position away. He squinted cautiously through a gap in the rockpile. He could see no immediate way of getting away. Perhaps when dusk fell he might be able to make a run for it and hope to find his horse, but against three men it was more likely that they would be able to move in on him through the darkness.

Suddenly the noise of three more shots blasted through the air. They came from a hillock to the right. Prayer cursed and rolled deeper into the cache of stones around him. It sounded as if reinforcements for the bushwhackers had arrived, shortening the odds against him. The latest shots were heavier than the first ones had been. They sounded as if they came from a Henry rifle. The initial flash of panic over, Prayer stopped burrowing into the boulders as he realised that the latest shots had not been directed at him. He was sure that they had been aimed at the main wall of the mine shaft.

Carefully the marshal raised his head. Two more shots exploded across the site. He saw huge slabs of stone go spinning viciously away from the wall of the shaft under the impact of the heavy calibre ammunition, almost obscured by clouds of dust. He wondered what the unknown marksman was doing. Then he heard the sound of rumbling from within the abandoned tunnel as the noise of the shots caused the debris of years to start falling from the roof. The rumbling increased to an explosion of noise. The exterior wall shook and then slabs began to fall on to the debris below, where the three bushwhackers were concealed. The three men stood up amidst the hail of falling rock and fled to one side of the hill to avoid the landslide.

Prayer was so surprised that it took him several seconds to level his Winchester and let off three rapid shots. The first two missed but the third caught one of the fleeing men in the leg. The ambusher fell with a cry, but struggled to his feet and limped off after the other two round the corner of the mine. In a moment Prayer could hear the sound of horses' hoofs disappearing into the distance.

Cautiously the marshal stood up. The landslide was dying away, the noise diminishing to a series of unearthly murmurs. He waited for the man who had caused it to walk forward through the clouds of dust. No one appeared. Prayer seemed to be alone.

Slowly the marshal walked off in search of his horse. His mind was buzzing with speculation. It looked as if Wade Jericho and his men had ridden ahead of him to pick him off as he passed the abandoned mine. But someone had come to his rescue, flushing the bushwhackers out of position by deliberately starting the landslide with the shots from his heavy rifle.

Briefly Prayer wondered who his unseen benefactor could have been. Then he dismissed the speculation from his mind. He had more immediate matters to worry about. It looked as if he had incurred the wrath of Wade Jericho and his gun-slingers and that they were determined to avenge the death of Brett Henry in Trail's End.

5

THREE men were waiting impatiently in the back room of Pa Kennedy's saloon shortly before midnight. The fat, slovenly form of Pa Kennedy was slumped over a table, a half-empty bottle of whisky before him. Mayor Ellcott was standing at the window, anxiously scanning the dark street. At another table, conspicuously apart from Kennedy, was the upright, well-clad, portly figure of Brannigan, the owner of the town bank. He seemed nervous and conspicuously out of place in the dingy drinking den. A solitary oil lamp on the bar cast a fitful light over the room.

"He's late," said the mayor anxiously, coming away from the window.

"He'll be here," said Kennedy contemptuously, refilling his glass with an unsteady hand. "He wants to do business with us."

Brannigan pursed his lips. "This is all most irregular," he said severely. "We could have met at the bank in business hours."

"The kind of business done in business hours ain't worth a pitcher of warm spit," said Kennedy. "If Jericho says he wants to see us, we'll wait on his convenience. We need him a hell of a lot more than he needs us."

"Nicely put," said a voice from the shadows. "I can see that you're a man who gets to the heart of a matter. Good evening, gentlemen. I'm sorry to have kept you waiting."

The three members of the Town Council whirled round. Standing in the doorway leading to the main saloon was the imposing figure of Wade Jericho. At his shoulder was the impassive half-breed Gradey, the trail cook.

"How did you get in here?" asked a startled Kennedy, almost knocking over his glass. "I locked the front door."

"Gradey and I have broken in and out of better places than this, if I may say so," observed Jericho. The big man turned to the half-breed at his side. "Go outside and watch the place," he ordered quietly. "If anyone approaches let me know."

Gradey nodded and disappeared wraith-like into the gloom. Jericho advanced into the room.

"Is one man enough to cover the saloon from outside?" asked Pa Kennedy nervously. "I can find some more hired hands, if you like."

"Gradey's enough," said Jericho confidently. "He's been with me a long time. Why, Gradey's a regular army all by himself."

Carefully Jericho lowered himself into a chair. His eyes took in the other men in the room.

"I'm glad you got my message and could make it," he said. "Which of you is Mayor Ellcott?"

"That's me, Mr Jericho," said the flustered Ellcott. "Good evening to you, sir. This is Mr Kennedy, the saloon owner, and Mr Brannigan, the proprietor of the town bank."

Jericho nodded. "And you're all members of the Town Council?" he enquired. "Let's get down to the bottom of the deck. Between you do you have enough influence to swing the votes of that council?"

"I believe so," said Ellcott, looking for reassurance to the other two men. "Under certain circumstances, that is."

"Hell, yes," cut in Pa Kennedy disgustedly. "If we say jump they ask how high."

"I'm glad to hear it," said Jericho. "I don't believe in dealing with middle-men. That can lead to a wholesale waste of time, which is something I don't have at the moment."

He stood up and walked behind the bar and examined the labels on the bottles of whisky stacked on a shelf. His nose wrinkled in contempt. Pa Kennedy pulled himself to his feet with an effort and stood swaying unsteadily before he lumbered over to the bar and reached down to produce another bottle.

"This here's the special stuff," he explained, blowing the dust off the neck.

Jericho scrutinized the label on the new bottle. He did not look overly impressed.

"It'll do," he commented, pouring some of the contents into a glass and walking back to the centre of the room.

"I wanted to see you three because I'm going to bring more business to Trail's End than you've ever dreamed of," he said sharply. "If things go right I'll bring even more trade here. I aim to make three more drives over the next year. Not only will I bring my own longhorns across the Jericho Trail, I'll trail-boss for two more Colorado spreads as well, maybe more. That means I'll be bringing close on five thousand head of cattle a year to the rail-head. I don't have to tell you what that will do to the town."

"And I suppose you will get a percentage of every head you get through?" said Brannigan cuttingly.

"That any affair of yours, bank manager?" asked Jericho softly, eying the portly man without affection.

"No, no, none," said Brannigan hastily, and fell silent.

"We surely appreciate what you intend to do, Mr Jericho," said Ellcott eagerly. Kennedy grunted assent, and even Brannigan recovered sufficiently from his confusion to give a stately inclination of his massive white head.

"I ain't doing it for you," said Jericho flatly. "I'm doing it for Trail's End. And that means I want a stake in the town."

"What kind of a stake?" asked a puzzled Ellcott.

"I want to buy land here," said the rancher. "Mr Brannigan, I believe you've foreclosed on half a dozen properties in the town and a couple of small spreads outside. I want to buy them off you. I also intend making other purchases as well in the fullness of time."

"That might be arranged," replied the banker cautiously. "At a price, of course."

"My price," said Jericho harshly. "If I'm going to make this town I want to own a good part of it. You'll take the price I offer you when I get paid for my cattle. Turn me down and I'll take my next drive into Dodge or one of the new towns along the line. You know what will happen then. Trail's End will curl up and blow away like leaves in a dust bowl."

"But this is blackmail!" gasped an outraged Brannigan.

"It's business," said Jericho matter-of-factly. "I want those deeds. There's nothing to stop you three buying other properties in the town yourselves, now you've got the inside information. The four of us can grow rich together."

From the suddenly animated expressions on the faces of the other three it was plain that the same point had occurred to them. Brannigan was looking particularly thoughtful.

"Something might be arranged," he murmured.

"Good, then I'll come in and look the deeds over tomorrow," said Jericho. "As soon as I've been paid off by the cattle buyers I shall want to deposit the money in your bank for a few days. Will it be safe there?"

"Safest strong-room in the state," replied a scandalized Brannigan.

"It had better be. All right, in the meantime there's just one thing to get straight. I've got two days to look after my steers before the train gets here. That means I need my hands, and I need 'em happy."

"No problem at all," said Pa Kennedy. "They'll be right welcome in Trail's End."

"The same way Brett Henry was welcome?" rapped the rancher. "Your marshal shot him down like a dog in the street."

The other three exchanged nervous glances. "That was a mistake," gulped Ellcott. "Marshal Prayer — "

"Marshal Prayer is young," said Jericho. "You only see straight ahead when you're young. I don't want him crowding my men over the next two days."

"He won't," said Pa Kennedy hoarsely. "I can guarantee that. John Prayer won't give you no trouble at all."

"I'm glad to hear it," said Wade Jericho grimly. "That boy's tougher than he looks."

"Don't hold the rest of us too light neither, Mr Jericho," rumbled Pa Kennedy, suddenly aggressive. "Reckon we can handle ourselves in an emergency as well." He paused and then added proudly, "Me and Ellcott here was there when we called out the Night Riders and shot 'em down like dogs in the street out there."

"Is that a fact!" asked Jericho, coolly unimpressed. "The way I heard it, most of you hid behind the marshal you had here at the time. Seems to me that's something you're good at in Trail's End — letting other folk do your dirty work for you!"

Pa Kennedy opened his mouth to reply angrily, but thought better of it and muttered incoherently to himself instead.

"This marshal you've got now," said Jericho, sipping from his glass. "Tell me about him."

"Ain't much to tell," shrugged Kennedy. "He's young. Thinks he knows it all."

"There's a hell of a lot more to him than that," replied Jericho sharply. "He rode out in to my camp to bring Henry's body back and he warned my men to mind their manners in town. I'd say he was something special in the way of lawmen to do that. I want to know about him."

"Hell, like Kennedy says, there ain't all that much to know," said Ellcott. "You could try Kate Richmond at the boarding house. Prayer's sweet on her. She might be able to tell you something about him."

"I'll do that," said Jericho. He glanced round the room. "Very well, gentlemen," he said. "I'm glad we have come to an agreement. Mr Brannigan, I will attend upon you at your office tomorrow. Good evening."

Jericho walked out of the room and through the saloon to the street outside. Gradey materialized out of the shadows.

"All right?" asked the half-breed.

"Not bad," said Jericho. "Not bad at all. Fetch our horses."

Gradey went down a side street and returned with their mounts. Jericho thought for a moment. He glanced down the street and saw a light in a downstairs window of the boarding house. He came to a decision.

"Take my horse back to camp and meet me outside the boarding house at nine tomorrow morning. Bring my go-to-town clothes with you when you come," he said. "I'll spend the night in town." A faint flicker of surprise washed across the half-breed's face. "Ain't like you to sleep in a soft bed till a job's over," he remarked.

"This job ain't hardly begun," said the trail boss. "There's a lot I need to know yet. Spending the night in town might be one way of finding out some of it."

He waited until Gradey had cantered off with the horses. Then he walked down the street to the boarding house. He climbed on to the boardwalk and tried the front door. It opened at his touch. Jericho entered the hall. The light was coming from the dining room. He tapped on the dining room door and went in.

Kate was sitting at one of the tables, going through some accounts in a leather-bound book. There was a pile of books at her elbow. She looked startled when she saw Jericho.

"Pardon me, ma'am," said the man. "I saw the light on, so I took the liberty of coming in. Is there any chance of a room for the night?"

Kate did not answer for a moment. Her assessing gaze took in the big man standing in the doorway, his massive shoulders filling the space. For a moment she was almost overwhelmed by the sheer magnetism of the newcomer. The word which came into her mind was power. This was a powerful man in every sense, one in complete charge of his life, an undoubted leader of others, yet with a calm self-assurance brought about by utter self-confidence. He made no effort to enter the room until she had responded to his opening remarks.

"It's rather late," said Kate. "I wouldn't have been up myself, but I'm waiting for one of my guests to return from the general store where he's trying to sell a line in fancy goods. I doubt he'll be successful."

"So do I," said the man dryly. "Not much demand for fancy goods in Trail's End at the moment, I fancy. I apologize for the lateness of the hour, but I've been at a meeting myself. My name is Jericho, Wade Jericho."

Kate stood up. So this was the famous cattle-driver, she thought. The man more than lived up to his reputation as a larger-than-life character.

"I'm Kate Richmond," she said briskly. "I'll be happy to have you here, Mr Jericho. How long will you be staying?"

"Just the one night. I haven't slept in a bed for longer than I can remember."

"Very well," said Kate. "Can I get you something to eat first?"

"I've eaten, thanks. If you could just show me my room."

"Of course." Kate walked towards the door. She saw that the big man was looking with interest over her shoulder. She turned to see what had attracted his attention. Jericho was looking at a tattered flag attached to the far wall of the dining room.

"It's the Night Riders' flag," she said with unconcealed pride. "It was taken from the leader of the Night Riders when they were shot down in the street outside more than ten years ago."

"How did it come into your possession, ma'am?"

To her annoyance Kate felt herself turning red. "It was given to me," she said. "By Marshal John Prayer after he shot down the leader of the Night Riders."

"He could only have been a child at the time," commented Jericho. "I take it that he was an admirer then. Is that still the case?"

"I hardly think that that is any of your affair, Mr Jericho," said Kate with asperity.

A smile of genuine warmth and charm creased the rancher's lined face.

"No more it is, ma'am," he agreed. "But he'd be mad if he wasn't — an admirer, I mean." He looked down at the table. "Don't often see books as part of the furnishings of a boarding house," he commented.

"*Hamlet*," said Kate, glancing at the book on top of the pile. "It's a play."

"I know," said Wade Jericho quietly. "I once saw McMaster Andrews play it."

Kate looked at the man in surprise. "Where was that?" she asked. "In San Francisco?"

Jericho shook his head expressionlessly. "A saloon in Virginia City," he replied. "He was touring with a fit-up company. He was drunk most of the time and he got most of his lines in the wrong order, but when he got it right you could see what all the fuss was about."

"You're an unusual man, Mr Jericho," said Kate.

"You're a cut above the average yourself, Miss Richmond. You may be wasted on Trail's End. I would figure you more as someone who would flourish in the culture of a large city, not in a small cow-town."

"I was born and brought up here," said the girl.

"And do you figure on staying here?"

"That depends."

Jericho raised an eyebrow. "On

Marshal Prayer?" She flashed a glance at him and the man raised his hands in mock defence. "I know, I know, that's none of my business."

"Quite right, it's not," said Kate, but she was smiling as she said it, almost overwhelmed by the charm of the man.

"If I may say so, you've made a good choice," said Jericho seriously. "From what I've seen John Prayer is the only real man in this town. It's a pity he's in such a dangerous line of business."

"Is he in trouble?" asked Kate quickly.

Jericho shrugged. "Trouble is a marshal's trade," he said. "Prayer knows that."

"He'll never do anything else," the girl told him. "It's all he ever wanted to be. He'll stand four-square behind anything he believes in."

"And you'll stand four-square behind him, is that it?"

"If he asks me to," said Kate steadily. "I'm not quite sure why you're here, Mr

Jericho, but if it's to look for any weak links in John Prayer, I'll tell you that as far as I'm concerned he doesn't have any. You and your men may find that out to your cost one day."

"Marshal Prayer is a fortunate young man to have such a charming and eloquent advocate," said Jericho, with a half bow. "Perhaps you could show me my room now? It's been a long day and I'm tired."

"Of course," said Kate.

She picked up the oil lamp and led the trail boss out of the room and up the stairs. As they climbed the stairs Jericho was frowning. It looked as if his fears about John Prayer had been confirmed. This was one lawman who was not going to back away from a fight. That was a pity, thought the trail boss; for a fight there almost certainly was going to be.

6

JOHN PRAYER sat alone in his office and pondered unhappily over what it was like to be an outcast. It was almost noon. The office was not usually as deserted as this. No one had been in to see him since he had returned from Wade Jericho's camp the previous afternoon. It looked as if the whole town had turned against him since he had gunned down Jericho's trail-hand and threatened to gaol any men on the drive who were wanted by the law. It was a weird feeling being ignored by the very people who had seen him grow up. Tod Washburn had warned him how lonely the job of marshal could be and now he was finding that out for himself.

He had spent much of his solitary wait in trying to puzzle out what could have happened at the old silver workings the previous afternoon. He was in little doubt that Wade Jericho and his men had bushwhacked him, even if he could not prove it. But who had been the unknown gunman who had caused the landslide with his heavy rifle and sent the trail hands packing? Not for the first time Prayer heartily wished that old Marshal Washburn was here to spell things out for him. He was in need of all the help he could get.

Prayer consulted his watch. Like it or not, it was time he took a duty swing through the silent town. Heaving himself out of his chair he checked his gunbelt and walked out into the sunlight. He let the sunlight play on his upturned face. At an unhurried pace he sauntered past the deserted stores.

Harlan Sullivan was sweeping out his general store as the marshal walked by. He was a thin, nervous, prematurely bald young man with a large wife and an even larger family. He dragged his broom to a rest when he saw the approaching marshal.

"Hear tell as you're set on keeping the trail-herders out of town, marshal," he greeted the other man in his high-pitched, nasal voice.

"Only the law-breakers," replied Prayer, slowing to a halt.

Sullivan gestured petulantly at the dusty shelves of the empty store behind him.

"Marshal," he said vehemently, "I'd give the Devil himself a friendly word and a fair price if he was to come and trade here, the way things are right now. We need those cowhands. They may be the dregs of the earth, but they'll have money in their pockets. We need that money. Trail's End is about a twitch and a turn away from being dead. Let 'em in, marshal please."

Having got that off his chest the store-owner turned his back on the other man and continued with his lethargic sweeping. Prayer continued stolidly on his way.

The only signs of life in the town were coming as usual from Pa

Kennedy's saloon. Pa might sell rotgut, but at least it was cheap. Prayer pushed his way through the swing doors and entered the long, dark, low-ceilinged room. There were about a dozen men at the bar or sitting at the tables, nursing their drinks and making them last. The noise of their conversations gradually died away as they saw the tall young marshal standing in the doorway. The silence hung heavy over the bar. Prayer nodded.

"Howdy," he said.

There was no answer. For a few moments Prayer surveyed the stony, morose faces turned in his direction. He could sense that something was going on and that it probably concerned him, but he knew that nobody was going to speak up while he was there. Behind the scarred bar Pa Kennedy mopped the swimming surface with a dirty rag and ignored him. Prayer hesitated and then left the saloon. He heard the sound of jeering laughter gradually mounting behind him as he walked on down the street.

His name was called. Prayer turned to see Doc Emblem limping after him. Emblem was an unshaven, vigorous man approaching seventy, incongruously dressed in a shiny black coat, a battered top hat and striped trousers which were too big for him. He was the nearest approach Trail's End had to a doctor. For years before he had settled in the town Emblem had been one of the frontier's saddleback doctors, uneducated, self-taught healers roaming from place to place, living with the Indians as much as with the whites and learning from their lore. The saddlebags of these doctors were packed with barks and herbs gathered on their travels and which they used instead of more orthodox ointments and medicines. In addition to healing sicknesses, Doc Emblem could extract bullets, sew up wounds, and on more than one occasion had amputated a limb using an ordinary hand-saw and a bottle of whisky, shared equally between doctor and patient. Prayer liked the old, self-appointed medical practitioner and knew that the town would be the poorer without his presence.

"Guess you've caught on that you ain't exactly the most popular fella in town," commented Emblem, catching up with the younger man and spitting a concentrated stream of tobacco juice on to the ground.

"I got that feeling," admitted Prayer.

"Can't hardly blame 'em," Doc Emblem pointed out reasonably. "You ever seen what happens when a place becomes a cattle town?"

"Can't say I have."

"Money happens, that's what. It pours in like it's coming in a river. The cowhands come, the honkey-tonk girls, the gamblers, the builders . . ."

"The doctors?" suggested Prayer gently.

Emblem bristled. "I ain't got no objection to competition," he said indignantly. "Bring in these fellas with their parchment certificates." He paused and winked. "Mind you, if they're coming to take my trade away they'd better be able to fight with their fists a bit, as well."

Prayer laughed. "I ain't got no objection to Trail's End growing, Doc," he said. "I'd welcome it. But it's my job to keep the town safe for the law-abiding folk against those who'd rule by the gun."

"I know that, son," said Emblem in a gentler tone. "But take my word for it, there ain't been a town in the West yet that's got bigger without blood-letting. And to my experience it's always been the lawmen who have gone first. The way things are looking now, if you go up against the trail-herders you'll be going on your own. I'd sure hate to be the one to pronounce you dead."

"I'll bear that in mind, Doc," said Prayer.

Emblem studied him intently. "No you won't," he said finally. "You're as hide-bound as Tod Washburn ever was. Must come with being marshal. Something in your water. Stubborn as mules, every last one of you. Leastways, the good ones are. All right, don't say I didn't warn you."

The old doctor turned and limped back purposefully towards the saloon and his drink. Prayer resumed his patrol. He turned a corner and came in sight of the boarding house. Prayer stopped outside the clapperboard building. Usually he ate at the cheaper Chinese place, but he did not feel like exposing himself to more ridicule so soon after his experience at the saloon. He decided to eat at the boarding house. There would be fewer people there. Besides which, he might catch a glimpse of Kate.

The dining room of the boarding house was almost empty as Prayer entered it and took his place at one of the tables, throwing his hat on to one of the hooks on the wall, next to the Night Riders' flag. There were two drummers with their bulging sample cases, their heads close together, exchanging experiences in a display of mutual self-pity, probably waiting for the stage to Dodge City, where they would report back to their companies on their lack of success.

Sitting by the window was the slight, bald figure of Grover Dart, the mortician, a permanent resident at the boarding house since the death of his wife a year before. The funeral director glanced up casually from his stew. He saw the marshal and gave an audible gasp, the spoon dropping from his nerveless fingers. His eyes still on Prayer, like those of a jack-rabbit transfixed before a snake, he groped ineffectually on the table for the spoon.

"Grover," greeted Prayer. "How are you?"

The mortician nodded weakly. Finally his questing fingers found the spoon and closed over it. With a visible effort Dart jerked his head away from the young man and attacked his food

110

savagely, directing all his attention to the plate. The resemblance to a rabbit was even more marked as the little man seemed intent on burrowing his way through the table to safety.

Kate came out of the kitchen and Prayer lost all interest in the mortician. The girl flushed as she saw the marshal, but recovered her composure at once.

"Marshal," she said evenly. "We don't often see you here. It's steak or stew. Which will it be?"

"I'll take the steak," Prayer decided. He remembered how well Kate and her Chinese kitchen helper fried the succulent steaks soaked in their own fat suet.

The girl nodded and turned to go back to the kitchen. With a spurt of courage he did not know he possessed Prayer reached up and touched her hand.

"I'm sorry you had to see the shoot-out yesterday," he said awkwardly.

The girl looked at him gravely. "I'd never seen a man killed before," she said in a subdued voice. "I hope I never see anything like it again. But it was your job, John. Just like keeping law-breakers out of Trail's End is your job."

For a moment the girl's fingers responded to his, and then she turned and swept out to the kitchen. A warm glow enveloped Prayer. At least one person in the town seemed to be on his side.

He had little time in which to savour the idea. A shadow fell across his table. He looked up with a start. Wade Jericho had entered the dining room and was walking across towards Grover Dart the mortician. The rancher was wearing a dark suit and was bare-headed. He nodded curtly as he passed the marshal.

Prayer returned the nod and watched with interest as Jericho sat opposite Dart and engaged him in conversation The little funeral director looked across the table at the trail boss and then swivelled his gaze across to Prayer.

Finally he pushed his half-eaten meal away, plainly losing all appetite for the stew.

Jericho spoke in a low tone tersely to the mortician, while Dart nodded miserably now and again. The rancher seemed to be asking questions. After a while he nodded, as if satisfied, and stood up and walked back towards the door. This time he did not even look at Prayer. The marshal waited until the big man had left the room before pushing back his chair and walking over to the table at the window.

"Better tell me what's going on, Grover," he said softly.

Dart ran a hand over his bald head and squinted up unhappily at the other man.

"It ain't none of my doing, Marshal Prayer," he whined. "It's business. I can't turn away custom now, can I? Ain't none of us in a position to do that."

"What sort of business are you aiming to do with Wade Jericho?"

pressed the marshal.

"Only sort of business I know," said the little man unhappily, beginning to sweat. He took out a handkerchief and mopped his face. "I'm burying the trail-hand from his drive who you shot yesterday. Jericho sent one of his hands in last night to arrange it. We're doing it in about an hour."

"Is that a fact," said Prayer slowly. "I suppose that means that the rest of Jericho's hands will be coming in for the funeral."

"Reckon so," gulped Dart. "They'll need to keep a couple of hands out on the range to look after the herd, but that's all." The little man rose agitatedly. "Now, if you'll pardon me, Marshal, I'd better go and finish off the arrangements."

Prayer nodded and walked back to his table as the mortician scuttled thankfully out. Kate came from the kitchen with his steak, potatoes and greens. She looked hopefully at the marshal but Prayer was too engrossed in his thoughts to take up their conversation. Quietly the girl put the plate down before him and went out of the dining room. Hardly noticing the food, Prayer cut up his steak with his knife and then transferred his fork to his left hand and started eating automatically.

He wondered which of the trail hands would be coming in to the funeral. If Billy Leif was with them then this would be an outright defiance of his orders of the previous day. He had warned Leif that the cowhand would be arrested once he crossed over the town boundary. Jericho and his men had had the best part of a day to make any plans, and they would probably be smarting from their ignominious defeat at the old silver mine. If Jericho was planning a showdown the streets of the town after the funeral would be as good a place as any.

At least one matter had been cleared up, he thought with satisfaction. He knew now why the patrons of the saloon had laughed after he had left that morning. The trail-hand who had come in from the range to arrange the funeral had obviously spread the word through the town that the marshal was about to be faced with a confrontation. That might not displease some of the townsfolk or members of the Town Council.

Prayer forced himself to finish his meal unhurriedly. Dropping a coin on to the table he walked out, looking at his watch as he crossed the room. The funeral should be under way any time now. Somehow he thought that he would be granted a good seat for the show.

Kate came out of the kitchen, wiping her hands on her pinafore as she did so. She looked anxiously at Prayer.

"Something's going to happen this afternoon, isn't it?" she asked.

"Could be," nodded Prayer.

"Well," said the girl, trying to hide her concern, "take care of yourself."

"Sure," said Prayer with a confidence

he was not feeling. He winked at her and went out.

Reaching his office he dragged a heavy chair out on to the verandah. Then he went back inside and loaded his Winchester rifle from a new box of shells. He checked the chamber of his Colt and went back out and took his place in the chair, toting the Winchester casually across his lap as he waited. Patiently he waited for the rest of the audience to assemble for the free show.

Slowly, as he had anticipated, the citizens of Trail's End congregated on both sides of the main street. The men and women said little as they waited but many speculative glances were cast at the young marshal sitting casually in his chair in the shade of his office wall, ignoring all that was going on around him. Amid the crowd he noticed the saturnine figure of Doc Emblem. The doctor was carrying the old black bag in which he kept what passed for surgical instruments in his practice.

Soon after one o'clock in the afternoon the trundling of the wheels of the funeral cart could be heard. Grover Dart always used an old mud-wagon for his business. This forerunner of the stage coach, with no springs, was stripped down to its bare essentials. It was pulled by four aged, plodding mules. Dart sat on the box in a dignified manner, holding the reins, with his apprentice, a fifteen-year-old called Charlie, at his side. Both men were in dark suits and were bareheaded. Behind the driver's platform, on the pared-down flat body of the cart was a rough coffin, hastily constructed overnight.

To the rear of the mud-wagon rode Wade Jericho and nine of his men. Only the rancher was in a suit. The trail-herders wore their working clothes. Each man carried a gun. In the middle of the group was Billy Leif. The unshaven stocky man grinned triumphantly at Prayer when he saw that the lawman had noticed him.

As the slow-moving expedition neared the marshal's office no one in the crowd made any effort to watch the mud-wagon. All eyes were on the marshal to observe his reaction. The procession drew level with the marshal's chair. Slowly Prayer began to raise his hand. There was an audible intake of breath from the fascinated crowd. The sneer vanished from Leif's face, to be replaced by a grimace of wild uncertainty. Prayer continued his movement and tipped his stetson in mock-respect to the coffin.

A shudder of mingled relief and disappointment rippled through the crowd. Leif glared vindictively at the marshal. Jericho, who had missed none of the byplay while seeming to stare straight ahead, turned his head and allowed his questioning glance to ripple over Prayer. Prayer made no response as the small procession passed by him towards the cemetery exposed to the elements at the top of the rise.

Cheated of their expected action the

crowd broke ranks and streamed after the procession. Most of its members cast puzzled looks at the marshal as they ran past, but no one questioned him as he sat immobile, still staring ahead as if lost in thought, his Winchester back in his hands.

For the best part of an hour Prayer sat patiently outside his office without moving as he waited for the burial to be completed and the mourners to return. The afternoon sun had edged appreciably across the sky before he heard the crowd straggling back down the hill. Jericho and his men on horseback led the throng.

Unhurriedly Prayer stood up and walked out into the middle of the street, cradling his rifle in his arms. Wade Jericho reined in his horse. His trail-hands pulled to a halt behind him. The crowd on foot pressed forward and surrounded the tableau in the centre of the street.

"State your business, Marshal," said Jericho quietly.

"Funeral all done with?" asked Prayer.

"You know it is."

"That's good," said the young marshal. "Wouldn't want it said that I wouldn't even let you bury your dead in the town."

"You killed him. We've buried him," said Jericho impatiently. "I'm still waiting to hear why you've stopped us."

"Law business," said Prayer. "Had to come." He indicated Billy Leif with the barrel of his Winchester. "I told that man not to come into Trail's End, unless he wanted to be arrested. Looks like he disregarded me. I'm telling you now, Leif, so you'd better pay me full attention. Get off your horse slowly and keep your hands in plain sight all the time. I'm holding you for murder in the town gaol until somebody comes for you from Wyoming."

For a moment the excited crowd surged forward to get a better view of the proceedings. Then it began to press back as it became obvious that Leif was unwilling to dismount from his horse. Jericho stared down coldly at Prayer.

"There's ten of us, marshal," he said distinctly. "Think you can take ten men?"

"I'm not looking to take the rest of you," said Prayer. "Only got paper on Leif. The rest of you are welcome in town. I'm calling upon you all to uphold the properly appointed law in Trail's End. Leif's under arrest."

Billy Leif pushed his horse past the other mounts until he was sitting next to Wade Jericho.

"This is the second time you've faced us down, lawman!" he shouted, his face red with fury. "You won't do it again!"

Prayer levelled his rifle at the killer's stomach. "Get down off your horse and hand over your gunbelt," he said. "I won't tell you again."

Leif looked desperately at his companions for support. "Are you going to take this?" he shouted. "Let's run him down."

The trail-hands looked to Jericho for a lead. The rancher was staring at Prayer through narrowed eyes. Finally the big man nodded.

"He's got the drop on you, Billy," he said. "That's plain for all to see. Get down and hand over your gun."

"To hell with that, and to hell with you too, Jericho!" screamed the incensed Leif, trying to control his bucking horse. "We ain't on the trail now. I make my own decisions."

The stocky man reached for his holster. Prayer tensed his finger beginning to squeeze on the trigger of the Winchester. Jericho forestalled him, moving with lightning speed. The rancher's huge gloved hand lashed out in a sideways motion, catching Leif across the face. The gauntlet smashed against unprotected skin and bone with tremendous power. Leif screamed and toppled from his horse to the ground, where he lay dazed, bleeding freely from the nose and mouth.

Prayer swooped forward and prodded

the semiconscious trail-hand to his feet, removing his Colt from his gunbelt as he did so. He dug the man hard in the ribs with the barrel of the Winchester.

"Inside!" he ordered.

His eyes unfocused, Leif stumbled uncertainly into the marshal's office. Prayer prodded him forward into one of the cells and kicked the barred door into place after him. Taking a large key from a hook on the wall he locked the cell door and walked back out on to the verandah, where the crowd was standing in a stupefied silence, hardly able to believe what it had just witnessed.

"That's all there is, folks," shouted Prayer. "Nothing left to see. Show's all done finished. Go about your business peaceable."

The excited mob broke up into small chattering groups and began to drift away down the street. Jericho and his cowhands did not move. Prayer looked up at the big trail boss.

"Much obliged," he said. "Mighty

public-spirited of you, Mr Jericho."

"Leif's a fool," said the rancher curtly. "It didn't suit me to get involved in a public shoot-out this afternoon. You would have killed Leif if I hadn't taken a hand, I know that. I want Leif alive. But watch your step, marshal. That's twice you've crossed me in two days. Ain't many men left alive who can say that."

Abruptly Wade Jericho spurred his horse off down the street. His bemused followers cantered after him. It was a sign of Jericho's control, thought Prayer, that not one of them had questioned their leader's brutal treatment of Leif. Prayer could not fathom out why the rancher had come to his aid and defused the situation in the street so effectively.

It was lucky for him that he had, thought the marshal, moving out of the sunlight back into the gloomy office. He felt drained and empty now that the action was over. Leif was sitting on the bunk in his cell, holding his head in his hands. He looked up savagely as the marshal entered.

"I'm going to kill you, Prayer," he promised with chilling vehemence. "When I get out of here the first thing I'm going to do is kill you."

Prayer ignored the outlaw. His next move should be to telegraph Wyoming and get a peace officer sent over to pick up the wanted man, he decided. He had better walk over to the railroad office and see the telegrapher.

Before he could move he heard the clatter of footsteps on the verandah outside. Porky Flynn put his grizzled head round the door. He was Tod Washburn's former deputy, an overweight man in his early sixties.

"Mayor Ellcott wants to see you down at the saloon," he said. "Says it's important."

Prayer nodded and moved towards the door. He could telegraph Wyoming after he had seen the mayor. "Reckon you can mind the store until I get back?" he asked.

Flynn had already dropped his considerable bulk into the marshal's chair, with a familiarity born of long practice.

"Sure thing," he said confidently. He glanced contemptuously at the sullen Leif. "When I wore a badge we went up against real gunmen, not trash like this," he said dismissively. He returned his attention to the marshal. "I saw you go out against those trail-herders just now," he went on. "Old Tod couldn't have done it better. Hell, I couldn't have done it much better myself!"

The boost given to him by the veteran's words lasted Prayer until he reached the saloon. Pa Kennedy's ramshackle establishment was packed to its swing doors, with drinkers spilling out in to the street. The men made way respectfully for the marshal as he entered the saloon. Prayer stopped just inside the doors, blinking to accustom his eyes to the poor light.

The drinkers were standing three deep at the bar, discussing what they had seen in the street a few minutes earlier. At one of the tables Wade Jericho was sitting with Mayor Ellcott and Pa Kennedy. Most of Jericho's riders were drinking at other tables. For the saloon to be this busy Prayer suspected that Jericho must be paying for the drinks. The noise in the room gradually died away as the drinkers noticed the marshal at the far end of the saloon.

Mayor Ellcott stood up and hurried over to Prayer, his hand extended and a false smile on his face.

"Thanks for coming by, Marshal Prayer," he said quickly. "I surely appreciate it. On behalf of the Town Council I want to congratulate you on your performance this afternoon. What you did took a lot of grit."

"Just doing my job, Mr Mayor," said Prayer quietly, wondering what the other man was leading up to.

"You sure showed that Billy Leif," said the mayor. "Yes sir, now everybody knows that there's law and order in this town and nobody bucks it. That'll give Leif something to think about the next time he's tempted to ride into Trail's End."

"Just a minute," said Prayer, sensing trouble behind the honeyed words being directed at him. "What do you mean? Leif's in gaol, and that's where he's staying until the Wyoming lawmen come to collect him."

"Now don't fly off the handle, John," said Ellcott anxiously. "What we've got to look at here is the broad picture, so to speak. Leif isn't important, and to be fair he's committed no crime in Trail's End. The Town Council has had a very full and frank discussion about this with Mr Jericho, bearing in mind that it was Mr Jericho who stopped Leif drawing on you and bulldogged him for you. We've decided to fine Billy Leif fifty dollars for disorderly conduct, which Mr Jericho has paid in full. We'd be much obliged if you'd release Leif into Mr Jericho's custody, just as soon as you can."

"You want me to let Leif go?" asked Prayer incredulously.

"Got to admit it," roared Pa Kennedy in the background, slapping his fat thigh. "Our marshal's as bright as a fresh-minted silver dollar. You don't have to draw him no pictures."

There was a roar of sycophantic laughter from the crowd. Prayer went red. He looked past the guffawing drinkers to Wade Jericho. The rancher was sitting erect and detached from the others, taking no part in the general merriment but regarding Prayer with a sombre gaze beneath beetling brows. So that was why Jericho had overpowered Leif, thought Prayer. He knew that he was going to be able to pay for the gunslinger's release before he left town that afternoon. It had been a clever move. There was no doubt about it. He had been out-smarted by the older man.

"Better get back to your gaol, Marshal," cackled Pa Kennedy. "Town Council's given you an order, and after all we pay your wages."

The saloon-owner started to laugh until he saw Prayer's gaze on him. To cover his unease Kennedy picked up his glass of whisky and drank quickly. The fiery liquid went down the wrong way and the saloon-owner began to cough.

"If you release Billy Leif you'll be throwing this town wide open to Jericho and his men," said Prayer desperately to Mayor Ellcott. "Can't you see that?"

"Now, now, John," said the mayor soothingly. "You're overreacting. Sure Mr Jericho's men may want to let off a little steam while they're waiting for the cattle train to arrive. There's no harm in that. Mr Jericho has promised to reimburse the town for any damage done. And you know how much we need his business in this town."

The assembled drinkers around them shouted their agreement. Pa Kennedy staggered unsteadily to his feet and placed a hand on the shoulder of the impassive Wade Jericho.

"We're proud to have Wade and his herders in Trail's End," declared the saloon-owner, his speech slurred. "And if you don't like it, Marshal, you sure as hell know what you can do about it."

Prayer gazed about him. Everywhere the drinkers seemed to be jeering and laughing at him. He knew that there was only one thing that he could do. He nodded. Slowly he reached for the tin star on his chest and unpinned it. He dropped the badge on to the beaten earth floor of the saloon.

Silence fell in the crowded room. Slowly Wade Jericho rose to his feet. He stared across the saloon at Prayer. There was a glint of mixed triumph and amusement in his eyes. He rose and shouldered his way across the saloon towards the door. As he went out he spoke for the first time since Prayer had entered the room.

"Drinks all round for everybody," said the rancher.

7

JOHN PRAYER stood over the desk in his office, shovelling the contents of the drawers into a burlap sack. Several hours had passed since he had dropped his star on to the floor of the saloon. Since that time he had been wandering aimlessly through the streets of the town, a red haze before his eyes.

He was furious and sad in about equal parts. He had given up the only job he had ever wanted, one for which Tod Washburn had started training him since he was a boy. Deep inside he knew that he had been right to resign. Wade Jericho had manoeuvred the Town Council into making his job untenable.

Porky Flynn, the acting deputy, looked on uneasily, not wishing to cross the young man while he was in his present truculent mood. He had heard what had happened back in the saloon earlier that afternoon. The news had spread rapidly all over Trail's End that the town no longer had a marshal.

"You want me to let him go?" asked Flynn, indicating Billy Leif, who was asleep on the bunk in his cell.

Prayer shook his head. "I'll hand him over to the Town Council, or his boss when they get here," he said, not looking up.

Flynn shrugged. "I'll be on my way then," he said. He hesitated. "I'm sorry about what happened. You were on your way to being a good lawman."

"So long, Porky," said Prayer, not meeting the other man's eyes and continuing with his packing.

The former deputy went out. Then the door opened again. Prayer glanced up, wondering what Flynn had forgotten. Kate was standing just inside the doorway. She was looking concerned.

"I've just heard what you did," she

said breathlessly. "Why?"

"I didn't have any choice," Prayer told her. "The Town Council didn't want a marshal; it wanted a pet dog. I don't come to heel so easy."

"I know that," said the girl quietly. "So what are you going to do now?"

"Haven't rightly thought about it," admitted Prayer. "Town marshal's the only job I've ever had. Didn't hold that down too long neither. I'd better start looking for something else that pays upwards of a dollar a day."

"You can come and stop at the boarding house until your luck changes," offered Kate. "You'll get three squares a day."

"No thanks," said Prayer decisively.

"Why not?" asked the girl.

Prayer looked up from the sack he was still packing. "Time I come calling for you at the boarding house it'll be to take you to a social, not asking for a handout," he said in a tone that brooked no discussion.

The girl took his meaning and

nodded. "Very well," she said. "In that case I'll be waiting for you, John Prayer." She thought for a moment and then went on in a rush, "John, there may be some who'll change their attitude towards you when they find out you're not the marshal any more. I won't. I'm not interested in what you do. It's what you are I'm concerned about."

She had gone before he could reply. Prayer knotted the top of the sack together. It was less than half full. He had not been around long enough to accumulate much in the way of possessions. Still, if Kate meant what he thought she did, maybe that was of little account. It looked as if he was going to have to reassess a lot of things in his life.

In the cell Leif groaned in his sleep and then opened his eyes. He stared blankly at the ceiling. Then he stood up and walked over and held the bars of his cell.

"Don't bother to tell me that this

gaol can't hold you," said Prayer indifferently. "You're getting out because you got friends in the right places."

A variety of expressions passed over the outlaw's face. Then he spat. "Had second thoughts, did you, Marshal?" he growled. "Don't make no difference. I'm still coming for you when your turn the key in that lock."

"I'll be here," said Prayer. "You can bet on it."

The door of the office was kicked open. Wade Jericho came in, followed by three of his men. Prayer picked up the key to the cell and went over and unlocked the door. Leif shouldered past him and looked round.

"Where's my gun?" he demanded.

Prayer walked over to the desk and took the outlaw's Colt from one of the drawers. He skimmed it across the surface to Leif. The other man picked it up eagerly and thrust it into his holster. He swaggered over to Prayer.

"Now it's you and me," he breathed.

Wade Jericho sighed. "Leif," he said

sadly, "sometimes you embarrass me."

The gun-slinger looked bewildered. "What do you mean?" he asked indignantly.

"He's given you your Colt back," said the rancher, as if talking to a child. "How about the shells?"

Comprehension dawned. Leif tugged his Colt out of its holster and examined the empty chamber. Prayer picked up a handful of cartridges from the surface of the desk and threw them on to the ground in front of Leif.

"In case you haven't worked it out the way Mr Jericho has," he explained, "if we have a difference of opinion, I draw and fire. On the other hand, you have to pick up the shells, load and then fire. There's a difference."

"About ten seconds' worth, I'd say," agreed Jericho dryly.

Leif glowered at Prayer and then turned on his heel and strode furiously out of the office. Jericho looked at his three cowhands.

"Go with him and keep him out

of trouble," he ordered. "Make sure he doesn't come back in here. You can have another couple of hours in town. Then I want you back on the range, so that Tommy and Luke can come in for a spell. I've already paid off Kilcannon and Martin, so you'll have to share the extra work between you."

Obediently the men followed Leif out. Jericho walked over to the marshal's chair and sank into it. He saw the sack containing Prayer's meagre possessions and raised an eyebrow.

"You didn't have to hand in your badge," he said calmly. "All you had to do was cut my boys a little slack."

"I was ready to do that," said Prayer stiffly. "All except Billy Leif. He was wanted."

"And that made all the difference to you, didn't it?"

"Mr Jericho, you don't seem to catch my drift. Billy Leif was wanted by the law."

Jericho swung his legs up on to the

desk. "Boy, you sure tread a narrow line," he sighed.

"It's the way I was brought up, I reckon."

"So what do you intend to do next?"

"You're the second person to ask me that this afternoon. I've got a few dollars saved up. I reckon I'll stick around."

The rancher's eyes narrowed. "I wouldn't recommend that," he said sharply. "Without that badge to hide behind you'll be mighty vulnerable. It won't just be Leif and his sidekicks. There'll be a lot of men in this town with a grudge against the law as well. They'll come crawling out of the woodwork now you're no longer a peace officer."

"Reckon that's my problem."

Jericho eased his legs back to the ground and stood up. "Reckon it is at that," he acknowledged. "Pity though. For a kid you were a good lawman. You used your head. You remind me of another young peace officer just starting out over at Ellsworth, name of Wyatt Earp." He shook his head with mock sadness. "I don't know what the West is coming to. The law's being run by a bunch of sassy boys with brains."

"Not in Trail's End any more it ain't," Prayer pointed out with a touch of bitterness.

"Ain't that the truth," said Jericho softly. He moved towards the door, passing the younger man. "I don't expect you to believe me," he said, "but I meant you no harm. I just couldn't have you out-thinking me in front of my boys. I need Leif and the others for two more days, until the cattle train gets here with the buyers. And they need me just that long as well. I can't pay any more of 'em off until the cattlemen pay me for my steers, just give 'em a little spending money is all. So the next three days could be a little noisy, what with my herders itching to spend their trail money when it gets here. Those

141

men are some of the toughest I ever come across, that's why I recruited 'em for the drive. But even if I appreciate 'em, I don't have to like 'em. So long, son."

The room seemed oddly empty after the charismatic big man had left. Prayer took one last look round. Then he picked up his Winchester and the burlap sack and stepped out on to the street. He unhitched his pinto and swung into the saddle. Unhurriedly he headed down the street past the saloon and stores, ignoring the curious glances being directed at him by those he passed. The last time he had ridden down the street, he thought sadly, he had been the marshal, with all that meant. Now, as far as the citizens of Trail's End were concerned, he was less than nothing. It was a long fall in a short time.

He rode about a mile outside the limits of the town until he approached the small, neat frame house on the hill overlooking a stream branching off from the main river, which had been his home for so many years and which Tod Washburn had left him when he died.

Something did not seem right. There were two horses hobbled outside the house. Prayer frowned. He did not recognize either mount. He wondered where the riders were. He heard the sound of raucous laughter coming from round the side of the house. Quietly Prayer slid out of the saddle a hundred yards from the house, and covered the intervening ground on foot cradling his Winchester. The men down the side of the house were making so much noise that they did not hear him approach until Prayer was upon them.

There were two of them. Prayer recognized them as having been with Wade Jericho when the funeral procession had ridden through the town earlier in the day. They were both big, leathery and unshaven, typical wild cowhands. They had obviously been drinking for most of the afternoon. At their feet was a tub of whitewash. One of the two men was just finishing painting the word LAWMAN laboriously in large scrawled letters on the wooden wall of the house.

They both heard Prayer at about the same time and whirled in surprise and alarm to meet him, reaching too late for their guns. Their arms froze when they saw the menacing barrel of the Winchester only inches from their noses.

"Howdy, boys," snarled Prayer. "Artists, eh?"

One of the two trail-herders tried to bluff it out. "Only funning, mister," he said uneasily. "No harm meant."

"Sure," said Prayer. "Only I've got a problem with that." He paused and an edge of venom chilled his tone. "This house was built by a man who was ten times better than anything you two could ever be, and I don't like to see it brought down by saddletrash!"

His grip on the Winchester tightened. The trail-herder's eyes widened in fear as he realized what the other man was going to do. He raised his hands to protect his head. Prayer reversed the rifle in his hands and smashed the stock full into the face of the cowhand. The man dropped like a stone and lay still on his back, his features disappearing behind a sudden gush of blood. Prayer turned on the other man.

"Make your play," muttered the cowhand. "You've got the drop on me."

"Not any more," said Prayer simply, throwing his Winchester to the ground. The cow-herder blinked stupidly, as if he could not believe his luck, but without hesitation drove hard with his right shoulder at Prayer, at the same time bringing up his foot in a vicious kick. The younger man had been expecting this. He swayed back and then released a mighty overarm left which caught the cowhand on the side of the head and sent him staggering back against the wall of the house. Prayer ducked his own head and followed up with a volley of blows to his opponent's body, causing the trail-herder to groan aloud. Desperately the cowhand tried to fight back, but he was slower than Prayer and had been drinking hard all afternoon. He did not come within a mile of possessing the cold fury of the former marshal at the desecration of his home.

The cowhand was no coward and did his best to stand up to his opponent. For several minutes the two men stood toe to toe, exchanging fierce punches but soon the trail-herder stopped punching and was reduced to trying to defend himself with flailing arms as he retreated, stumbling back along the side of the wooden building. Finally Prayer nailed him against the corner of the house and with a final flurry of punches sent the trail-herder slumping almost senseless to the ground.

Prayer staggered back, sucking his skinned knuckles and aware that his clothes were soaking wet with sweat.

Reaching down he picked up his Winchester. He used the barrel of the rifle to prod both dazed and bleeding cowhands to their feet. Grimly Prayer indicated the whitewashed slogan on the wall of his house.

"Now clean it off!" he ordered between puffed and bleeding lips.

Without looking at him the two battered trail-herders started to wipe down the side of the house.

8

JOHN PRAYER was up early the next morning. He threw wood into the gaping mouth of the pot-bellied stove and lit the fire, balancing an iron pot over the flames as they began to roar. He cooked himself several plates of grits, ground some beans into dust and drank a mug of black coffee. When he had finished eating and drinking he went out and fed and watered his horse in the small corral running down to the stream. Then he walked back into the house and carefully oiled and loaded his Colt.

He had been thinking hard long into the night, sitting by the light of an oil lamp at the deal table in the living room, beneath the stiffly-posed photograph of Marshal Washhurn and his wife Meg on the wall. At first he had brooded on his misfortune in coming up against the shrewd machinations of Wade Jericho and being cornered into handing in the badge which had meant so much to him. With an effort he had thrown off his mood of self-pity and settled down to try to work out what he should do next.

The easy answer would be to ride out of Trail's End for ever. He could travel south-west. There would be plenty of work down Arizona way as a deputy for a young lawman in such growing towns as Tucson or Phoenix. But Prayer knew that he was not going to leave the town in which he had grown up so happily and which had provided him with a fresh start when he had been abandoned by the wagon-train as a child. All right, so the Town Council and most of the citizens had rejected him. They had been blinded by greed and the prospect of the wealth that cattle-drives would bring to the town. One day they would come to their senses, and if Prayer was any judge of character, sooner rather than later the honest folk in the town would be in need of the protection of a fast shooting arm against Jericho and his herders, even if he was no longer their marshal. In particular Kate would be there in the centre of any trouble. He knew that the independent minded girl would refuse to leave the town, no matter how bad things became. There was no doubt in his mind that before long the cowhands from the trail drive would bring bloody mayhem to Trail's End, and that when that time came he had better be there to use all the skill that Tod Washburn had taught him, to try to combat the hell-raising which surely was going to follow. His roots were here and he was prepared to give his life for the town and its people if he had to.

Prayer decided that the first thing to do that morning would be to ride out to the grazing land and get some idea of what Jericho and his men were doing. The cattle train was due in a day or so. The rancher would then pay off his men, and after that the trouble would probably start.

Prayer buckled on his gunbelt and tied the thong securing his holster to his leg. He walked outside and saddled his horse and began to ride out towards the range in the bend of the river where Jericho was fattening his cattle.

After a mile or so he swung wide, forded the river and took his mount up into the foothills which skirted the far side of the Clear and looked down on the grazing lands by the water's edge. From here he could watch what was going on below without being observed. He gentled his horse along the rise and then stood looking down on the herd and men scattered below him. It was a peaceful scene. After the dangers of their epic drive Jericho and his men now had little to do except prevent the longhorns from straying too far before the cattle train arrived from the east. That meant that only three or four trail-herders would be needed at a time to keep an eye on the herd.

The rest could loaf around the site or drive into town.

At the moment, apart from the few outriders out on the horizon, most of the trail-herders were squatting round a wood fire drinking coffee. Prayer dismounted and sent his pinto back down the far side of the slope, while he lay on his stomach in the long grass on the top of the hill and watched the scene in the camp. He waited there for an hour or so, observing the comings and goings of the cowhands about the site. He saw Wade Jericho once, when the big man came out of his dug-out in the side of the hill and poured himself a cup of coffee from the pot on the fire, before going back into his shelter. The trail-boss ignored the other men scattered on the ground.

Billy Leif seemed to have the most to say for himself as the cowhands lazed around the fire, although a rangy red-haired trail-driver also took his full share in the conversation. Prayer could also pick out the two men he had forced to scrub the side of his house the previous afternoon. They seemed quieter and more subdued than the others in the group.

Soon after ten o'clock a group of six of the herders, including Billy Leif and the red-head, began to saddle up their horses, laughing and joking, and prepare to ride out of the camp. Prayer guessed that they would be going into town and decided to shadow them to see what they did in Trail's End. As the small group of horsemen rode out of the camp he reclaimed his pinto and rode parallel above them along the brow of the hill, keeping back among a row of cottonwoods along the top of the rise.

To Prayer's surprise, about a mile after they had left the camp the six riders took a swing away from the trail leading to the town, and swam their horses across the river, until they were on the same side of the Clear as he was. He was still able to keep them in his sight, although he could not guess where they were headed.

Thirty minutes later he began to guess the destination of the men below him. They were heading for a cutting in the hill where the railroad track came in from the prairie and squeezed through the overhanging bluffs, going up a gradient before leaving the hilly area and heading over open ground again to Trail's End. The riders stopped by the cutting through the hill and examined the area with care, circling their horses and then regrouping to talk eagerly among themselves. Finally they turned their horses and began to ride across the open land in the direction of Trail's End.

Prayer watched them go, trying to figure out the reason for their detour. They might have been looking for strays but the cowhands did not seem that conscientious to him. Prayer became so engrossed in his meditations that he did not hear the other man ride up behind him.

The first he became aware that he was not alone was when he heard the crack of a shot and the dull thud of a slug burying itself in the trunk of a cottonwood tree a yard to his left.

Prayer fought his bucking horse and dragged it round to face the direction of the shot. Twenty yards away, half-obscured among the trees, Wade Jericho was straddling a big dun, a smoking Colt in his hand.

"You did half good and half bad," drawled the rancher to the surprised and mortified Prayer. "You did good to track Leif and the others from up here, but you did bad to let me sneak up behind you."

"I didn't figure on anybody riding shotgun for Leif," admitted Prayer. "I should have looked back, I guess."

"Hell, I wasn't guarding Leif and the others," exploded Jericho with a sardonic laugh. "I was as curious as you were to see where they were going. It was only after I followed 'em out along the ridge that I saw you was ahead of me."

"Is that why you fired at me?" asked Prayer ruefully.

"Just wanted to make sure I had your full attention," said Jericho mildly.

"You've got it," said Prayer.

"Good," said Jericho, shelving his revolver. "Let's go back to camp and have ourselves some coffee."

The rancher turned his horse and led the way back down the side of the hill, across the river and into the camp-site. Apart from Gradey squatting rolling a cigarette by the side of his empty cookpot they seemed to be the only men on the site. Prayer supposed that the remaining trail-herders were out with the cattle.

The two men dismounted and walked over to the glowing embers of the fire. Jericho picked up two discarded tin mugs from the ground and filled one with coffee from the pot, handing it to Prayer before he filled the other mug for himself.

"It's good," he said, gulping down the scalding liquid. "I only brought the best on this trip. Best coffee beans, best cook, best trail-hands."

"Much obliged," said Prayer, trying the coffee. It certainly had a lot more flavour than he was used to. He tried to get to grips with the situation. Jericho could have shot him dead up on the ridge and left his body to moulder under the trees. Instead he had invited him down for coffee. Whatever else the rancher was he was certainly neither a conventional nor an easy man to figure out.

"You've decided to stay on in Trail's End then?" said Jericho.

"I've given it some thought," nodded Prayer. "I was brought up here. Don't see no reason to move on."

Jericho swallowed the last of his coffee and threw the dregs on to the fire. He dropped his cup to the ground.

"Got kin in these parts?" he asked.

"I was brought up by the last marshal and his wife. They're both dead now."

Briefly Prayer explained the details of his upbringing. Jericho heard him out and nodded.

"Never had anywhere I could call home myself," he said.

"Hear tell you've got a big spread in Colorado," said Prayer.

"Just land and stock, not what you could call a home. Comes a time when a man needs a real place to call his own." Jericho was silent for a few moments, lost in a reverie. Then he recovered and fumed to the younger man. "Don't hold those herders of mine too light, just because you've been lucky this far," he warned abruptly. "Those ordinary sons-of-bitches are some of the coolest back-shooters you could ever wish not to meet. Leif rode with Colonel Lawrence when he went fifty miles behind the Yankee lines during the war, and that redheaded slat McGiver was one of the James boys' gang in their first bank raids. Ain't hardly a man on the drive who ain't done his fair share of riding and robbing in his time. And most of them served with the Union and learned extra fancy ways of killing there. They ain't overfond of Johnny Rebs neither. That's why I recruited them, because they're so no-account. Those low-life sons of bitches brought the cattle across wilderness country no other man had ever managed."

"And now you've thrown a nest of rattlesnakes into Trail's End," said Prayer, placing his empty mug on an adjacent rock.

Jericho shrugged. "Reckoned I'd worry about that when the time came," he said. "You going back to town now?"

"How did you know that?" asked Prayer.

"Because it's what I'd do if I was in your shoes," replied the rancher. "Don't turn your back on any of 'em. Leif's a real sidewinder; he'll kill you without thinking twice about it. And I hear tell you hurrahed two more of my boys outside your place yesterday. They said you came at 'em like a spitting wildcat. It's getting so as most of my herders have got cause to draw on you when they see you."

Without a word Prayer walked across to his horse.

"What do you intend on doing in Trail's End?" Jericho asked his retreating back.

"I don't know," said Prayer. "Stomp on a few rattlers, maybe." He looked down at the other man from his saddle. "Why," he asked, "do I get the idea that you aren't too concerned if I get the drop on a couple of your boys?"

A shade of surprise passed over the rancher's face, to be replaced by a reluctant grin. "Just leave me a couple to drive the longhorns into town on Friday, that's all I ask," he said.

"Tell me something," Prayer asked curiously. "Just what were Leif and the others doing down by the railroad track back there?"

"Well, I'll tell you," said Jericho comfortably. "Those killers may be

160

mighty tough, but they ain't too smart in the head department. I've been waiting for the best part of a couple of days for them to catch on about the track beneath the bluff."

"What about it?" frowned Prayer.

"Well, stands to reason, if you're going to make an effort to rob the train when it comes in, that's the best place to make your move."

"You reckon Leif is going to stop the train?" gasped Prayer.

Jericho shook his head. "He was thinking about it. That's why I was keeping an eye on him. If I was going to hold up the train, that would be where I'd do it, as it slows down to approach the gradient. Plenty of room to hide in the trees below the bluff."

"A train robbery," said Prayer slowly. "I never figured on that one."

"It ain't going to happen," said Jericho with assurance. "I could tell from the way Leif rode off. It would be too difficult. That train is tucked up as tight as a can of beans. It'll be a lot easier for Leif to get the cattle money once it's paid over to me in Trail's End. At least that's what Leif figures. I'll be seeing you, kid."

Jericho turned and walked over to the waiting Gradey. In turn Prayer urged his mount forward. He rode out of the camp and then let the pinto have its head as it headed at a leisurely pace towards the town. Matters were beginning to clear up in his own mind, at least as far as Wade Jericho was concerned. He knew now beyond any doubt that the rancher's main intention was to use him. He was beginning to appreciate the sheer extent of the devious approach adopted by the powerful rancher. The outlaws Jericho had gathered together for the dangerous cattle drive could be replaced by the rancher. It would not worry Wade Jericho at all if Prayer were to take on some of the gunslingers. If Prayer were gunned down in the street it would make no difference to the trail boss. On the other hand, should Prayer get lucky and manage to kill one or two of the gunslingers first, that would leave fewer men to pay off when the cattle-buyers arrived with their money.

Prayer continued to turn the situation over in his mind as he got closer to Trail's End. He had surprised the rancher when he had let it drop that he was on to Jericho's scheme, and it had given him some satisfaction to come out even against such a famous character. But that did not alter the basic situation. Over the next two days, one way or another, Trail's End was going to be placed in considerable danger at the hands of the trail-herders. He could not think of a single man in the town who would stand up to Leif and his men unaided once they got started. That left it up to him, whether he was still marshal or not.

He reached the town and left his mount at the livery stables, ignoring the sour scowl of the man in charge as he took the reins of the pinto from the former marshal. Then he walked down the main street to the boarding house, trailing his Winchester. Those he passed on the way either nodded curtly or paid no attention to him at all. One or two of the drifters contemplated directing a derisive remark or two at the one-time lawman, but there was something about the set of Prayer's jaw and the width of his shoulders which dissuaded them and sent them scuttling on their ways.

He reached the shaded verandah of the hotel. Kate must have been watching him because she came out at once, a broom in her hands. It was a Saturday and school was closed. Prayer tipped his hat.

"Mind if I set here awhile?" he asked formally.

"You're very welcome, John Prayer," said the girl formally. "Can I get you something to eat?"

"Maybe a cup of coffee later in the morning," said Prayer politely. "Until then I'll be just fine."

He settled in the rocking chair a little to one side of the door of the boarding house, from where he had a good view of the main street in both directions. Kate looked puzzled but could see that Prayer was in no mood for idle conversation. She nodded and went back into the house.

Prayer leant back in the chair, his eyes half-closed but his mind alert. He waited for about thirty minutes. Then Leif and the other trail-herders he had shadowed from the ridge came rowdily out of the livery stables and started swaggering up the street towards the saloon. As they passed the boarding house they saw Prayer waiting in the shadows of the verandah. Their laughter stopped at once and the men stood uncertainly in a knot in the street, facing him. Leif was the first to recover from the general surprise. He walked slowly over towards the boarding house.

"What are you doing here?" he demanded harshly.

"Sunning myself," answered Prayer calmly.

Leif controlled himself with an obvious effort. "One day soon," he promised viciously, "you and me are going to sort things out. Jericho's told us that you mustn't be hurt. Time the cattle train gets here and Jericho will pay us off, your luck plum runs out. After that he don't have no say in the matter. That's when I'll come looking for you, Prayer."

"You'll likely know where to find me," said Prayer, not raising his voice.

"Just keep it in mind, Prayer, you're not the marshal any more," shouted the red-headed McGiver from the crowd of trail-herders. "Best keep out of our way, kid."

"And you boys," said Prayer serenely, settling his rifle more comfortably in his lap, "had sure as hell better keep out of mine."

Leif spat and turned and walked back to the others. The group started walking noisily down the street towards the saloon. Prayer watched them go. He was aware of Kate coming out of the boarding house and standing behind him.

"What's going to happen, John?" she asked in a small voice.

"First the boys are going to get drunk," he replied. "Then they'll get nasty. After that," he shrugged, "there's no way of telling."

"Shouldn't they be stopped now before anyone gets hurt?" the girl asked with concern.

"Ain't nobody to stop them."

"Of course; we don't have a marshal any more." The girl put a soft hand on the man's shoulder. "You're sitting here to look after me, aren't you?"

Prayer grinned up at her. "Heck no," he scoffed. "Whatever put that notion in your head? Where else in town would I get a friendly word and coffee on the hour?"

The girl tried to smile but found it difficult. "I'll get out of your way," she said, turning to go.

Prayer nodded. "Might be better if you concerned yourself with chores about the house today at that," he said as lightly as he could. "It may not be so good out on the streets later on."

After the girl had gone back inside Prayer pondered on Leif's words. Jericho had warned his trail-hands not to tangle with him, yet Jericho had made it plain to Prayer that he would not object if the former marshal fought and killed some of the herders. It was a puzzle. Just whose side was the rancher on? His own, decided Prayer, and the big man was surely playing a mighty devious game. Well, the town would just have to take its chances, thought Prayer. He would do his best, but he had one main objective that day. The only thing that mattered to him in Trail's End at the moment was Kate. As long as he was around she would be protected, he would guarantee that.

The rest of the morning and the first part of the afternoon passed slowly. Prayer continued to sit on the verandah, apparently completely relaxed but missing nothing of what was going on in the street. From the saloon he could hear the raucous laughter of Leif and the other trail-herders. From time to time various hopeful hangers-on would hurry into the saloon in the hope of free drinks, but judging by the way they returned quickly and disconsolately to the street it looked as if they were being disappointed.

It was at about three o'clock in the afternoon that Prayer heard the first fight break out in the saloon. The sound of angry shouts was followed by the splintering of furniture. Then two men Prayer recognized as employees of the livery stable were hurled out of the swing doors. They lay dazed and bleeding on the ground before staggering to their feet and limping off back to the stables. The noise of a brawl continued from inside the saloon. Unhurriedly Prayer stood up and walked along the street to the sound of the fighting.

For a moment he stood outside the saloon. He heard the sound of shots. Quickly he shouldered his way into the building. Leif, McGiver and two more of the trail-hands were leaning against the bar, drinking whisky and shouting encouragement to the other two trail-drivers who had ridden in with them that morning.

These two drunken cowhands were busily engaged in shooting up the fitments behind the bar. They had destroyed most of the bottles on the long shelf and had turned their slavering attention to the row of oil lamps placed in a row of alcoves. As Prayer looked on, the hail of fire from their revolvers sent the shattered shards of the lamps spinning through the air.

Pa Kennedy was cowering behind one corner of the bar, his great bulk quivering.

"That's enough, boys," he pleaded fearfully. "Come on now, you've had your fun."

The cowhands ignored him, looking for fresh targets. Kennedy looked over to the door and saw Prayer. Relief flooded over his fat, unshaven face.

"Marshal," he begged in abject supplication. "Please. You've got to stop 'em."

The cowhands followed the direction of his imploring gaze. They stiffened when they saw the tall, motionless figure of Prayer. Paying no attention to the cowhands Prayer walked across the room and sprawled across the bar, reaching for one of the bottles behind it. Carefully he poured a drink into a glass and savoured the burning liquid as it coursed down his throat.

"What this place needs," he said, staring at the ceiling, as if thinking aloud, "is some law and order." He drank again and placed a coin upon the bar. "Unfortunately, it don't have any no more, remember, Mr Kennedy?"

The trail-herders guffawed triumphantly. Kennedy gibbered incoherently. The two men who had been competing with their Colts picked up their revolvers again, looking for new targets.

"Don't forget the mirror, boys," Leif reminded them.

Pa Kennedy screamed with a mixture of terror and outrage and lurched forward as if to protect his most treasured possession. The two cowhands started firing wildly at the huge expanse of glass. Their bullets thudded into the mirror, cracking it beyond repair and causing great chunks to splinter and fall to the floor. Kennedy moaned and dropped to his knees over the wreckage.

"Let's get out of here," said Leif in disgust.

The trail-herders trooped towards the door over the debris. Kennedy looked up and shouted after them.

"You've got to pay for this!" he demanded.

Leif looked dangerously at Prayer to see if he was going to interfere. Prayer pushed his empty glass away.

"Best send for the marshal, Mr Kennedy," he advised ironically.

Leif looked speculatively at Prayer, as if trying to work out what the younger man was up to. Studiously Prayer ignored the outlaw's gaze. Leif gave up the effort to fathom the other man's motives, deciding that for the moment there were easier targets in the town. He laughed humourlessly as he led the other herders out of the saloon. Prayer cast a final look round at the wreckage and at Pa Kennedy trembling impotently at the corner of the bar. Then he followed the cowhands through the batwinged door out into the street.

He looked on as they conducted their campaign of noisy vandalism. At first a few onlookers assembled, but when the townsfolk realized the vicious nature of the trail-herders' campaign they disappeared rapidly back into the stores, leaving the main street deserted except for the cowhands and the watchful Prayer. At first the cowhands concentrated on shooting their revolvers in the air, but before long they were shattering the windows of the stores they passed. One store-keeper rushed out to expostulate, only to flee back into his store as half-a-dozen shells were aimed at his feet on the boardwalk.

"Yankee scum!" shouted one of the trail-hands.

Prayer followed in their wake, making a mental note of the damage being caused. Some of the townsfolk cowering in the doorways looked at the former marshal appealingly, but Prayer ignored them, his eyes intent on the drunken roisterers.

They reached the boarding-house and passed on by. Prayer relaxed. He stepped up on to the boardwalk and entered the house. As soon as he opened the door he had a premonition of disaster. The hall was empty. He hurried into the dining room. The room looked as if it had been hit by a hurricane. Tables and chairs were scattered everywhere. On the wall, where the captured Night Riders' flag had hung for over a decade was a bare patch. Trying in vain to overcome the fear in his heart he hurried back to the door.

"Kate!" he called urgently. "Kate, where are you?"

There was no reply. Quickly Prayer ran through the boarding house, shouting the girl's name as he threw open doors in a frenzy of apprehension. The only person in the house was Kate's kitchen assistant, a diminutive Chinaman, who shook his head fearfully and cowered against a wall when Prayer tried to question him.

Prayer ran out into the street. It was most unlikely that the girl would have gone anywhere at this time in the afternoon, especially after he had asked her not to leave the building.

He ran up the street towards the livery stable. Leif and the other trail-herders were about to mount their horses. They looked with hostility at Prayer as he stood fighting for breath in the entrance.

"Where's Kate?" he panted.

"What the hell are you talking about?" demanded Leif without interest, getting on to his mount.

Prayer seized the man's horse by the bridle and glared up at him. "Kate Richmond from the boarding house," he said urgently. "She's not there. Where is she?"

"I don't know and I don't care," retorted Leif, struggling for control of his frightened horse.

"If you've taken her I'll kill you," promised Prayer, doggedly retaining his grip on the bridle.

Leif glared down at him. "How the hell could we have taken anybody?" he asked violently. "We ain't hardly been out of your sight all day!"

With an effort he wrenched his horse's head free and rode out of the stable. He was followed at a gallop by the other trail-herders. Prayer had to jump back to let them pass. Then he turned and picked up his saddle and frantically began to fasten it on to the back of his horse.

9

MOST of the town had gathered angrily outside Mayor Ellcott's provender store, summoned by the banging of an iron bar on the forge in the blacksmith's shop, the traditional method of announcing trouble in the town. Other men were running across the street from all directions to join the jostling throng. Questions were being asked and incoherent answers shouted. Men were jostling to get to the front of the mob. On the boardwalk Ellcott was trying to restore some form of order so that his voice could be heard above the baying of the startled and angry people before him. Within a few minutes of the first sounding of the crude alarm there had been a mass exodus from all the buildings along the street. Occasional shards of conversation could be heard among the overall babble.

" . . . Shot the whole town up . . . "

" . . . Bust up the saloon and broke the mirror . . . "

" . . . Stole the Night Riders' flag from the boarding house . . . "

" . . . Ran off with Kate Richmond . . . "

" . . . They've taken Kate with 'em . . . "

" . . . Called us Yankee scum and lit out back to the grazing land . . . "

" . . . They've gone too far this time . . . "

" . . . Don't care how much money they bring into the town . . . "

"Hold it down!" begged Mayor Ellcott hoarsely. "Come on, will you? Let's have some order here. We all saw what the cowhands did in the street just now, and I can tell you that as mayor of this town I ain't going to stand for it. No, sir, they've gone too far. But what's this about Kate? Are we sure she's not here?"

"Ain't no decent woman going to venture out on to the street while those trail-herders are raising Cain, that's for sure!" cried a large, red-faced woman indignantly.

Before Ellcott could reply there was the sound of a horse cantering down the street towards the saloon. Everyone in the crowd turned. John Prayer was heading down the main street. He had fed and watered his mount and checked his ammunition while the crowd had been debating events. He did not spare a glance for the people outside the provender store.

"Wait a minute, John," called Mayor Ellcott appealingly. "Where you headed?"

"To find Kate. Where the hell do you think I'm going?" said Prayer unbendingly.

"We're just forming a posse. Ride with us, John, please," begged the mayor.

"I wouldn't ride with you if you was to give me a horse with six legs," said Prayer contemptuously, and continued on his way out of town.

He rode, his heart full of cold rage, until he reached the outskirts of the trail camp. Then he forded the river and urged his mount up the side of the hill overlooking the trail-camp. He hobbled his mount on the far side of the slope and then crawled on his stomach until he could observe what was going on in the bend of the river. The cowhands below were standing round uncertainly in groups. Even from this distance they looked agitated and uncertain. Prayer waited patiently for half an hour. Then what he had been waiting for happened. One of the trail-hands broke off from the others and ran for his tethered horse, mounting it and riding it hard out of the camp.

Prayer rose and ran back to his own horse, removing the hobble and mounting the pinto. The trail hand below was heading towards a fissure in the cliffs, where the railway track ran between the hills on its final approach to the town. Prayer managed to keep the rider in sight most of the time. The man below reached the gap, dismounted and sat down by the railway track. It looked as if he was waiting for someone or something.

Prayer hesitated. He was tempted to remain where he was and see who came along to join the cowhand, but he did not have enough time. He had to get Kate back quickly, and every minute was precious. Quietly he tied the pinto to the branch of a tree and then began to descend the slope.

He took a roundabout route so that there was no chance of the waiting man seeing or hearing him. Prayer concentrated on moving quietly, so that the waiting man by the railroad track would not hear him, half creeping, half slithering over the grass of the slope. He reached the bottom of the slope and paused to get his bearings. The cowhand was about twenty yards away, sitting by the side of the railroad track, smoking a cigarette. Prayer took his Colt from its holster and levelled it as he crossed the intervening ground.

"Hold it right there, mister," he said menacingly.

The trail-herder froze, the cigarette drooping between his lips. Prayer came up behind him and removed the revolver from the other man's holster, throwing it on to the ground behind him.

"Get up," he said. "Slow and easy."

The other man did as he was told and turned to face Prayer. He was a half-breed of about fifty, with dark hair streaked with grey and worn long. He regarded Prayer unemotionally, his hands up, level with his shoulders.

"What's your name?" asked Prayer.

"Gradey," replied the half-breed tonelessly.

"Well, Gradey, I'm going to ask you some questions. Answer 'em wrong, or don't answer 'em at all and you're a dead man. You understand that?"

"I understand."

"For your sake I hope you do. Where's Kate?"

"I don't know what you're talking about."

With the speed of a striking snake Prayer brought the barrel of his Colt sweeping across Gradey's face, breaking the skin and sending the blood gushing down the half-breed's cheek. Gradey took an involuntary step backwards and raised a hand to his wound, but did not cry out.

"In case you don't know it, Kate is the girl I intend marrying," Prayer told him. "Killing you won't bother me worth a damn if it leads me to getting her back."

The half breed shook his head sulkily and did not reply. Before he could move Prayer crashed the barrel of his revolver against the other side of his unprotected face. Blood gushed from the second wound. Gradey shook his head like a wounded and cornered animal. A spray of blood flew from the second wound.

"If hurting you doesn't do it, I'll start shooting your fingers off, one at a time," promised Prayer. "I ain't got much time to spare, mister."

He could see no change of expression in the other man's face but a hint of apprehension appeared in his eyes. Prayer cocked his Colt and raised it.

"Wait!" said Gradey.

"I'm waiting," said Prayer.

"Jericho's got the girl," said Gradey. "He said he was going to go in to town and take the flag, just as a sign to you Johnny Rebs. The girl saw him taking it down, so he brought her along with him, in case she raised the alarm."

"How do you know this?" pressed Prayer.

"He rode into the camp with her not long ago. He said he was going to take her somewhere safe and leave her there. He didn't want to come back to the campsite. He told me to ride out here and wait for him.

"Where has he taken Kate?" snarled Prayer.

"I don't know," said Gradey. Prayer's

finger tensed on the trigger. The half-breed gave a pitiful howl. "Honest, mister, I don't know! Jericho wouldn't tell me." He gestured vaguely towards the north. "He's out there somewhere in the badlands with the girl."

Slowly Prayer lowered his revolver. It sounded as if the half-breed might be telling the truth. He cast about in his mind for the best thing to do. If he waited here with Gradey, Wade Jericho would come back eventually, but he would almost certainly be alone, and he might be made of tougher stuff than the half-breed and refuse to say where he had left the girl. He simply could not take the risk of losing any more time.

"If I find out that you've been lying, I'll come back and hang you from the nearest tree," he told Gradey, reversing his Colt and bringing the handle down with crushing force on the other man's head.

Gradey slumped to the ground and lay by the railroad track without a murmur. He should be unconscious for a fair period of time. Prayer hurried back up the slope and untied his horse, leading it gently down the slope back to the rail track. Gradey still lay inert on the ground. Prayer surveyed the area indicated by the half-breed before he had been knocked out. For miles stretched dry open plains, interspersed for as far as the eye could see with jumbles of large rocks and outcrops and occasional dustings of trees. It was desolate country, attractive only to coyotes and outlaws on the run.

Holding his mount by the reins Prayer inspected the ground. If Jericho had arranged to meet Gradey back here, this might have been the spot from which the rancher had started his journey across the plain with Kate. He had less than an hour's start, so any marks should be plain enough to see.

Even so it took Prayer ten minutes to find the first tracks in the dust. They were of two horses heading north; judging by their indentations one was more heavily mounted than the other. That looked like Jericho and Kate. Prayer mounted his horse and set off across the plain, keeping the tracks ahead of him

He rode steadily for the best part of an hour, stopping every so often to check the trail. Occasionally, when the ground became rocky, he lost the imprints of the horses he was chasing but always, sooner or later, he found them again and continued on his relentless progress.

It was mid-afternoon before he saw his first signs of any life. When he did it was not an attractive sight. Ahead of him was a small spread, not nearly big enough to deserve the title of ranch. The place was typical of many such poverty-stricken homesteads springing up in the state as men with no gift for farming tried to scrape a living from the soil. There was a small, crude, lopsided log cabin built on the bank of a muddy creek. An equally ramshackle barn had been thrown up to one side of the building. In front of the cabin was an ill-tended vegetable garden. A few scrawny cattle grazed morosely on the poor grassland surrounding the farm. The overall impression was one of grinding poverty and decay

Prayer pulled up outside the unpainted picket fence protecting the vegetable garden. He waited. After a few minutes the front door of the cabin was thrown open and a man sidled out, cradling a shotgun in his arms. He was thin, round-shouldered and emaciated, wearing old Levis and a collarless shirt which had once been white. The homesteader had not shaved for a week. The dispirited and beaten man in front of Prayer seemed in little better condition than the cattle he owned.

The man kicked the door shut behind him, but not before Prayer had caught a glimpse of a frightened woman and two or three ill-dressed and dirty children huddled together and peering at him through the narrow opening.

"Howdy," said Prayer pleasantly.

"The name's Prayer."

"State your business," said the emaciated man roughly tightening his grip on the shotgun.

"Maybe you can help me. I'm looking for somebody," said Prayer. "A big man and a young woman. Have you seen 'em?"

"No. Now ride on."

"That's funny," said Prayer. "I've been tracking 'em across the plain. Looks like they stopped here, got off their horses, maybe to water 'em. I find that kind of hard to take in."

"I mind my own business," muttered the homesteader. "Don't interfere in other people's affairs."

"The girl may be in trouble," Prayer told him. "I've got to catch up with 'em fast."

A bitter laugh emerged from the homesteader's dried lips. "Trouble?" he said harshly. "You don't know what trouble is until you've tried to farm through a drought. Those rains that came are too late to save my crops, mister, and I'm too far from the main river to profit from any floods."

He should have thought of that before siting his homestead in such a barren and obviously unsuitable area, thought Prayer. Aloud he said: "The girl was kidnapped,"

"Wish he'd taken my woman as well," said the homesteader tonelessly. "I wouldn't have stopped him."

"You have seen them then?" asked Prayer.

The homesteader pursed his lips judiciously, summing up his visitor. "Maybe, maybe not," he said. "You're keeping me from my work, and my time is worth money."

He stared through red-rimmed eyes at Prayer and said no more. Prayer reached into his pocket and produced a fifty-cent piece. He tossed it to the other man. The homesteader caught the coin effortlessly, bit it and transferred it to his pocket all in the same movement.

"There were two of 'em, like you said," he informed Prayer. "Well set-up tough-looking fellow, about forty, and a pretty young woman. They watered their horses and set off for Adobe Springs."

"Where's that?"

"About ten miles north-west of here. Only source of water out on the plain for a long way."

"Thanks," said Prayer. "All right if I water my horse at the spring before I ride on?"

"That'll be another fifty cents."

Prayer dropped the coin on the ground without a word and walked his horse to the spring. The homesteader picked up the coin without embarrassment and watched Prayer intently all the time the horse was slaking its thirst. He did not come near the other man but all the time the barrel of his shotgun never wavered. He was still standing listlessly in the vegetable garden when Prayer rode off towards the north-west.

Prayer resisted the temptation to urge his horse into a gallop. In this heat it would be asking too much of the animal. He kept going at a steady canter across the dusty plain. Once he even got off and walked his mount for the best part of a mile. He was not far from Kate now. When he found her it would probably result in a show-down between him and Wade Jericho. So be it, he thought grimly.

While he was still a mile away he could see the glint of water in the sunlight. The Springs formed a large lake of water almost entirely surrounded by trees and outcrops of rock. There were half a dozen adobe houses crumbling by the side of the water. These dwellings of sun-baked bricks made of earth and dried corn stems must once have housed hunters or prospectors.

Prayer tethered his pinto to a tree and proceeded carefully on foot towards the water, making use of the rocks and trees as cover. He saw Jericho and Kate almost at once. The rancher had built a fire and seemed to be cooking flapjacks over it in a heat-blackened pan. Kate was standing looking on. She seemed unharmed. Prayer took his Colt from its holster and stepped out of the trees.

"All right, Jericho," he said. "Put your hands up!"

Wade Jericho looked up calmly from the fire. "Hello, Prayer," he said. "You took your own sweet time getting here. I damn near laid a trail right across Kansas for you to follow."

Before Prayer could respond there was the ominous click of a pistol being cocked. He felt the cold barrel of the gun laid against the side of his head.

Slowly Prayer turned. He found himself staring into the swollen, baleful face of Gradey, the half-breed.

10

"THIS," said John Prayer in a voice shaking so much with anger that he could hardly control it, "had better be damn good."

"My flapjacks are always good," said Wade Jericho in a hurt tone.

"I didn't mean the flapjacks!" said Prayer, his voice rising to a half-shout.

The four of them were sitting eating round the wood fire by the side of the spring, all except the half-breed, who was nursing a swollen jaw in addition to the cuts on his cheek-bones, between directing spiteful glances at Prayer. Prayer and Gradey had holstered their revolvers. Kate was flushed and silent, avoiding eye-contact with Prayer. Only Jericho seemed fully at ease.

"I'll tell it from the beginning," offered Jericho.

"Go ahead," said Prayer tersely.

"Time I decided to drive my herd from Colorado to the rail-head at Trail's End six months ago, I knew I would need some pretty good men to come with me," said the rancher between appreciative mouthfuls. "By good I mean as hard as hickory and none too particular. Well, I got 'em. About a dozen, counting Gradey here, who's always worked with me. The men I signed on for the trip weren't the sort of men you'd take to a church social, but there was none better for moving a thousand head of cattle across hard land."

"They were outlaws," said Prayer. "Hired guns and murderers."

"Well, not to put too fine a point on it, yes," agreed the rancher. "And do you know something, that didn't worry me one damn bit. As long as we were crossing flooded rivers and bucking Indian attacks, there was none finer for my purposes. The way we went on that drive I didn't leave 'em much time to consider their outlawing ways and habits. Of course the position changed when we reached Trail's End."

"They went back to what they'd always been, you mean, Mr Jericho," said Kate seriously.

"Miss, you are as bright as you are beautiful," admired Jericho.

"Never mind that," said Kate automatically, but Prayer noticed with chagrin that the girl did not seem displeased with the compliment. "You always knew that they'd turn mean when they reached the town, didn't you?" she went on.

"I know a coyote will always be a scavenger, even if you shine his coat and call him a guard-dog," nodded Jericho. "It don't fool the coyote none. Only natural that Billy Leif and his boys would take up thieving again, just as sure as the sun rises and sets. You couldn't rightly expect anything different from them."

"And the only thing worth stealing within five hundred miles would be the money you were going to get for your cattle. You knew that as well," said Kate judiciously. She frowned, delicious little lines appearing on her alabaster brow beneath the rim of her riding hat. "You were taking a big risk with them."

"Something like that," said Jericho, scraping his plate. "I've always taken risks."

"All right," said Prayer, getting a little jealous of the way Jericho and Kate seemed to be taking a shine to one another. "So why did you do the things you did?"

"You tell him, Kate," suggested Jericho. "You seem to have figured it out just the way I did, only a lot quicker."

"Don't you see, John," said the girl eagerly, worrying the matter with the enthusiasm of a dog attacking a bone, "Mr Jericho knew that he would be getting thousands of dollars from the cattle buyers as soon as the train got here. He also knew that Leif and the others would try to steal it. He had to work out a way of keeping his money."

"And to do that I needed help," said Jericho, taking up the account. "That meant I had to get the people in the town on my side. Only there was no real reason why they should take any chances for a rich former Union major. I had to find some other way of getting 'em roused. Best way I could think of was to get 'em real riled up against us all. Only I couldn't stand apart from the others, so when you arrested Billy Leif, best thing I could do was knock him out to stop him shooting you, but I had to persuade the Town Council to take away your badge, else Leif and the others would know I was on to 'em."

"So you let Leif and the others come into town this afternoon, knowing there was no law in the town and that they would act up and get everybody's goat," said Prayer slowly. "Then you moved in and stole the Nightriders' flag and kidnapped Kate, so as the folk in the town would really get to hate the trail-herders." He glanced suspiciously at Kate. "Only when I got here you didn't seem so all-fired mad at being taken."

"That's because I wasn't taken," said Kate quietly. "Mr Jericho explained what he wanted to do, and I agreed to ride off with him to make it look as if I'd been kidnapped."

Prayer threw down his plate in exasperation. "Now why in hell did you do that?" he yelled.

"Because Miss Kate knows what's right for you, that's why!" Jericho bellowed back, losing his self-possession. "She was doing your thinking for you, that's what!"

The two men glowered at one another across the camp fire. Prayer picked up his plate again.

"Personally," Jericho went on in a calmer tone, "I think Miss Kate's much too good for you, but she seems to want you, so that's good enough for me."

"Mr Jericho," said Kate with icy

dignity, standing up, "when I decide that I want a man, as you put it, I am perfectly capable of telling him myself. I shall not need you to do it for me, thank you very much!"

The girl rose and strode away, disappearing into one of the adobe shelters. Jericho and Prayer watched her go, jaws agape.

"That sure got her riled up," said Jericho calmly. "That girl's got more sense in her little finger than you've got in your whole lanky body," he added.

"I know that," said Prayer. "What I don't know is how you persuaded her to ride out here with you."

"Because she wanted to keep you alive," said Jericho. "We both do. In fact you have no idea just how hard I've been trying to keep you from getting killed over these last few days."

Comprehension began to dawn on Prayer. "It was you, wasn't it?" he said. "It was you who rescued me when Leif and the others had me pinned down at the old mine."

Jericho nodded. "When you had the guts to ride out and face me down after you'd killed Brett Henry, I knew you were the man for me," he said. "If anyone was going to stand up to the trail-herders when they came for my money it would be you. What I had to do was to get the townsfolk so mad at Leif and the others that they would be ready to back you up in a show-down when the cowhands tried to rob me. Just like they stood by Tod Washburn when the Night Riders rode in all those years ago. So when I saw Leif and the others light out after you that afternoon you brought Brett Henry's body back, I followed 'em and pinned 'em down by the silver mine."

"But how did getting Kate out here help me?" asked Prayer.

"The way I saw it, if'n you stayed in Trail's End for the rest of the day, sooner or later you would come up against Leif or some of his boys. Sure as hell they would shoot you down. In the back if the other way didn't look too inviting. On the other hand, if you thought Kate had been kidnapped, you would ride out after her and be safe."

"How did you know I would find you?" asked Prayed dazedly.

"I gave you credit for some sense," said Jericho. "I guessed you'd hang around to see if any of the cowhands rode out to find me. I'd fixed it with Gradey here for him to let you tail him to the railroad and then for him to tell you where to find me after you had knocked him around a mite. Then I laid the most obvious trail I could, including letting that homesteader see us. I couldn't have done it much plainer if I'd drawn you a map and issued you an invitation."

Prayer looked at Gradey. "I thought Kate was kidnapped," he apologised shame-facedly. "I wouldn't have laid your face open else."

The half breed ran a hand over his disfigured face and grimaced in pain. He looked accusingly at Jericho. "You said he'd ask me questions and then likely tie me up when he lit out after you," he mumbled through swollen lips. "You didn't say nothing about him half taking my head off."

"Boy, was I ever wrong," said Jericho callously. "Man, this guy is a tiger. Must make you question your trust in me, Gradey."

Gradey scowled and was silent. Prayer stood up, trying to digest everything that he had learnt over the past few minutes.

"So what do you want me to do?" he asked.

"Back me and Gradey up when Leif and the others make their move tomorrow," said Jericho promptly.

"How can I back you up? I ain't even the marshal any more."

"I'll make you marshal again when this has blown over, if that's what you want," said Jericho impatiently. "In the meantime I'll pay you fifty bucks to throw in with us. You'll earn it mind. We'll be outnumbered three to one. However, fifty bucks wouldn't be a bad sum to start out on a marriage with — if you live that long."

"Will you shut up about me marrying," demanded Prayer.

"Sorry," said Jericho. "Well?"

"I won't do anything illegal."

"The thought never entered my mind," said Jericho with heavy sarcasm. "All I'm asking you to do is like as not get yourself killed. What's that compared with doing something against the law. Pardon me for even thinking such a thing."

"All right," said Prayer. "I'll do it."

"Good," said Jericho with obvious relief. "Now what I want you to do is — "

"Later," said Prayer, striding towards the adobe hut. "I got me some fences to mend first."

Kate was sitting on an upturned box as he entered the gloomy single room of the hut. She opened her mouth to speak. Prayer forestalled her.

"Let me have my say first," he abruptly. "I know what you've done and why you've done it. Maybe you should have told me first before you lit out with Jericho, but I know now that you did it in consideration of me. And I know that Jericho is right about one thing. I ain't nowhere near good enough for someone like you. But if you could bring yourself to overlook that, I never would. And I'd try for the rest of my life striving to improve myself to make myself somewhere close to fitting for you."

At first the girl shook her head as if she could not believe what she was hearing from the man's stumbling lips. Then radiance spread like a soft dawning sun over the girl's upturned face. "Oh John, I love you so much," she murmured, half-crying as she rose and threw herself into his arms.

They stood tenderly together for what seemed like a long time. Then they heard the sound of a dry cough coming from the doorway. They turned to see an impatient Wade Jericho.

"You two have got the rest of your

lives for that," he sighed. "As far as I can tell the cattle train will be here tomorrow morning, and I've got me a substantial investment to protect. Do you mind if I tell you my plan now?"

11

THAT evening most of the men in the town with the price of a drink in their pockets, and some who did not, assembled uneasily at the town saloon to discuss the events of the day. Soon Pa Kennedy and his two barmen were working busily behind the bar in the long, crowded room.

"Never had anything like this happen in Trail's End," fretted Mayor Ellcott, chewing the end of his moustache. "Not even in the war."

"Is John Prayer back yet?" asked one of the men in his group. "He won't give up easy. John's a fair tracker. If anyone could pick up a trail it would be him."

"No, John's still out there somewhere," said another man with feeling. "You're right about him. Best tracker and rider in the town. Ellcott, you were crazy to let him turn his badge in. This town needs some good law and order. We've seen that today."

There were rumbles of agreement from the dispirited men in the saloon. Ellcott looked round in vain for allies. Behind the bar Pa Kennedy shiftily avoided the mayor's gaze.

"The trail-herders didn't want him," said Ellcott weakly. "We needed their goodwill."

"To hell with the trail-herders!" shouted a voice from the back of the room. "They're Northerners, ain't they? Burnt the South to cinders in the war and now they've come back to tell us how to run our town. They've even stolen the Night Riders' flag and kidnapped one of our women. We may be poor, but we've got our pride. Are we going to stand for that?"

Roars of angry agreement filled the room and Pa Kennedy and his barmen scurried frantically behind the bar to meet all the orders as the men present fuelled their anger with more drink. There was so much noise in the saloon that at first Mayor Ellcott did not hear his name being called. It was not until an arm tugged at his sleeve that he saw Prendergast, the telegrapher, standing next to him. Prendergast was a dignified man in the peaked cap of a railroad employee.

"Message from the railroad!" he shouted. "Cattle train should be here by ten o'clock tomorrow morning. They want to start loading as soon as possible and head back for Chicago the same day. I've sent a messenger out to the camp-site to tell the trail-herders."

Ellcott nodded without much enthusiasm and crumpled the message form and thrust it into his pocket. He had an ominous gut feeling that unless he could do something about it, when the cowhands started driving the longhorns through the streets of the town the next day they would meet with a distinctly hostile reception.

★ ★ ★

A brief sliver of moonlight illuminated the trail for a moment as Wade Jericho, John Prayer, Kate and Gradey, the half-breed, approached the outskirts of the town. Each man was leading a spare horse which Gradey had taken from the corral at the camp-site without any of the out-riders with the herd noticing his stealthy approach. Jericho reined in his mount and turned to the others as they pulled up beside him.

"Right, Miss Kate," he said briefly. "You'd better not go back to the boarding house in case someone sees you, when you're supposed to be missing. You'd better go back and wait at Prayer's place. He shouldn't be too long. All right?"

Kate nodded and drove her horse off into the darkness. Jericho turned his attention to the others.

"You both know what to do," he said briefly. "We've got to make as much noise as possible without anybody actually seeing us. Use your pistols and your rifles. They've got to think there's at least a dozen of us attacking the town."

"But nobody gets hurt," said Prayer quickly. "We fire into the air, right?"

"Sure," said Jericho irritably, controlling his restless mount. "We've been through all that. Gradey, it's your job to get the livery stable alight, just like last time." He forestalled Prayer's objection. "They keep the horses out the back; they won't be harmed, and when it's all over I'll pay for any damage. You got the fixings, Gradey?"

The half breed nodded and indicated his saddle bag, which held two pitch-soaked wooden torches and a flint and tinderbox with which to obtain sparks to light them.

"It's a hell of a thing we're going to do," said Prayer in awed tones. "I can't hardly believe that we're even trying it."

A brief, savage smile twitched beneath

the rancher's moustache and then was gone.

"Amen to that," he replied.

★ ★ ★

In the saloon the drinkers were keeping the barmen as busy as ever. Many of the men were drunk.

Pa Kennedy took advantage of a momentary lull in the action at the bar to approach Ellcott stealthily.

"Hell of a mess we're in," said the bar-owner gloomily. "If we back the trail-herders we're going to get run out of town by our own people. If we go against the cowhands Wade Jericho will take his next cattle-drive to another rail-head, and that will kill off Trail's End. What are we going to do?"

Mayor Ellcott shook his head unhappily and drank some beer. "There's one way," he said after a pause. "It's a long shot, but it's all I can think of."

"Well, go on," urged Kennedy.

"Ain't no way the people here are ever going to take a shine to the cowhands, not after what they've done today," said the mayor. "However, they ain't going to spit in Wade Jericho's eye, not if he brings prosperity to the town."

"I don't get your drift," frowned the saloon-keeper.

"Well, the way I see it, we've got to cosy up to Wade Jericho, but let people see that we're going to clamp down on his trail-herders."

"How the hell we going to do that?" demanded Kennedy blankly.

"Maybe through John Prayer," said the mayor thoughtfully.

"Come again?" gulped Kennedy.

"Jericho admires Prayer, I could see that. They're two of a kind. Fighters. If we could persuade Prayer to become marshal again, he could maybe handle Jericho and keep him neutral, and still go up against the cowhands."

Kennedy gaped at the other man.

"Do you think Prayer could do that?" he asked.

"It's a long shot," admitted the mayor. "But have you got any better ideas?"

"Me? No, of course not," said the saloon-owner quickly. "So what are you saying? We've got to make Prayer marshal again?"

"Looks like it," said Ellcott. "Couldn't make us any worse than we already are."

"I suppose you're right," said Kennedy. "You always did do the thinking for the both of us."

"Too much thinking, sometimes," said the mayor.

"What's that supposed to mean?" frowned the saloon-keeper.

"Sometimes," said Ellcott wistfully, "just sometimes I wish that we did less thinking and just did what ought to come natural."

"Like what?"

"Like if someone threatens our town we just get up and fight back. That's

214

what Tod Washburn used to do, and it's what John Prayer would have done, if we'd let him. But no, we always had to be thinking what was right in the long term." Ellcott stared straight ahead at the ruins of the mirror on the wall, his reflection distorted in the shattered glass. "I've just about had enough of thinking. I want to fight for the town the way people like Washburn and Prayer fought for it when the Night Riders came here."

The saloon-owner began to speak but stopped. He cocked his head to one side. "What can I hear?" he asked sharply. "Sounds like gun-shots to me." He raised his voice above the din in the saloon. "Shut up, all of you!" he bellowed. "Listen!"

Gradually the noise died away. In the distance could be heard the sound of rifle shots. The men in the saloon exchanged apprehensive glances and then jostled to the window to peer out into the dark main street.

"We're being raided!" shouted

a frightened voice. It's the trail-herders!"

★ ★ ★

At the far end of the street John Prayer pumped shots rapidly into the air from his Winchester, at the same time controlling the two horses in his care. To his right Wade Jericho was emptying his Colt into a tin sign outside the blacksmith's shop, causing a horrendous reverberating noise. Carefully Gradey lit his torch and hurled it through the open doors of the livery stable on to the straw heaped inside. There was a violent rushing sound and then the interior of the barn burst into flames.

"Get away from the light!" shouted Jericho. "They mustn't see us!"

The three men urged their six horses up and down the length of the street, shouting and firing their weapons in to the air. The noise was indescribable. Two members of the posse, braver or more curious than the rest, came cautiously out on to the boardwalk from the saloon, illuminated by the light inside the building. Calmly Jericho aimed his Colt and sent splinters of wood flying from one of the wooden supports of the saloon, less than a foot from the heads of the two men. In unison they turned and dived back inside. No one else came out as the occupants of the saloon cringed at the window, trying to make out what was happening in the dark street.

For ten minutes the three men and the six horses outside hurrahed the town mightily, firing round after round into the air and shouting incoherently, all against the flickering backdrop of the burning livery stable. Finally Wade Jericho reined in his horse and reached down to take something from his saddlebag, which he plunged into the ground at the feet of his mount.

"Reckon they'll know we've come a-calling," he grunted. "This should give 'em something to think about. All right, let's get out of here fast!"

Prayer and Gradey spurred their mounts and followed the big man at a gallop down the street and out of the town. It was another five minutes before the first men ventured apprehensively out of the saloon. Most of them dashed down towards the livery stable. The owner of the hardware store opened up his premises and started distributing buckets. The members of the posse formed a chain and, passing the buckets filled from the horse-troughs, started fighting the fire.

As Mayor Ellcott and Pa Kennedy emerged more slowly from the saloon the moon came out from behind a cloud and lit up the street. The two men stopped and goggled at something just ahead of them.

"What the hell is that?" growled Kennedy.

The two men advanced on the object and stood regarding it reflectively. Ellcott reached forward and picked it up. Attached to a pointed stick was the tattered and holed flag which had been stolen from the boarding-house that afternoon.

"I don't believe it!" grunted Pa Kennedy after a pause, in mingled awe and horror. "The Night Riders have come again!"

★ ★ ★

On the outskirts of the town Jericho and the other two reined in their horses. Jericho was grinning.

"Went as sweet as a nut." he chuckled. "The way they'll be telling it by now, they were attacked by fifty wild men. Gradey, we'll take the spare horses back to the corral before anybody misses 'em."

"What do you want me to do?" asked Prayer.

"You know what to do," Jericho told him. "Just ride back into the town. After the way we've just softened them up just about everybody in Trail's End will be looking for a saviour. You're the nearest they've got to that item in these parts. I'll see you both tomorrow."

Jericho spurred his horse away in to the night. Gradey gathered together the riderless mounts and without a word set off back in the direction of the trail camp. Slowly Prayer rode back into the town. He did not approve of what Jericho was doing, because he felt that all the rancher was doing was using people, but he felt that the best thing he could do for the time being was to go along with the big man's ingenious plans.

By the time he reached the main street the fire in the livery stable had been put out and the townsfolk were assembling dazedly in the main street. Pa Kennedy was examining the ground in the light of the moon.

"Can't tell how many of them there were," he grumbled. "Judging by these tracks and the noise they was making when they shot up the town, I'd say at least twenty."

"Probably twice as many as that," said

another voice amid general agreement.

They heard the sound of Prayer's approaching horse and looked up. The crowd began milling round the former marshal.

"What's been going on here?" asked Prayer, trying to look innocent.

"We've just been raided, that's what," complained Pa Kennedy. "The whole town's been shot-up."

"Who by?" asked Prayer, keeping a straight face.

"Reckon you can take your choice," muttered the saloon-owner. "It was either the ghosts of the Night Riders coming back to haunt us, or them Union boys in the trail camp have started the war all over again!"

12

BY noon of the following day Wade Jericho and his trail hands started driving the herd through the streets of Trail's End. The trail was lined with spectators. Most of them had never seen so many cattle at one time before. The main street of the town had been left free for the cattle drive but the boardwalks were packed with onlookers. Prayer noticed how sullen the townsfolk were. There was no attempt to cheer the advent of the trail-herders. Too much had been said and done over the past few days to give the occupants of Trail's End any reason for liking their visitors. What should have been a big day in the life of the town had turned into a watchful, antagonistic event.

The longhorns milled between the wooden stores, urged forward by the trail-hands. At the end of the street was the newly constructed rail depot and its adjacent stock pens. The train was waiting, its cattle trucks stretching back behind the engine and solitary passenger car. The engineer and his fireman were already taking on water and wood for the return journey.

John Prayer stood watching from the boardwalk, waiting for Jericho to acknowledge his presence. For the moment the rancher was too busy. Three cattle-buyers in well-cut Eastern suits and derby hats were waiting on the raised wooden platform of the depot. Slightly behind them were two large, tough-looking men armed with shotguns. These would be the hired guards, thought Prayer. There was probably a third in the passenger car looking after the money.

It took several hours to fill the stockades with the lowing longhorns, and then the trail-hands began the sweaty task of urging the beasts up the wooden inclines into the waiting cattle trucks. Jericho stood to one side with a notebook, jotting down the number of longhorns being loaded. The cattle-buyers did the same on the other side of each truck.

It was evening before the last animal was loaded on board and the trail hands were able to relax. Jericho jerked his head at Prayer and walked off towards the passenger car of the train with the three buyers.

"Wait out here," Jericho ordered, as he went into the car with the buyers and their guards.

Patiently Prayer waited for the trail boss to emerge. He would already have negotiated a price with the buyers by telegraph. The only things left to check were the number and condition of the longhorns.

Half an hour later Jericho emerged from the passenger car, looking satisfied. He was carrying two large, heavy canvas bags. He handed one to Prayer and retained the other.

"Don't carry it in your gun hand,"

he ordered laconically, and set off down the street in the direction of the bank.

Behind them the train gathered a head of steam and began to move out of the depot with its cargo of longhorns. The large crowd which had been watching the loading process slowly dispersed and began to trail up the main street. The cowhands tethered their mounts and began to congregate on Jericho and Prayer. Automatically Prayer felt for the handle of his Colt.

"You want a hand with that there money, Mr Jericho?" leered Billy Leif, grinning wolfishly.

"We can manage," said Jericho equably. "Me and Prayer to carry it; Gradey to ride shot-gun on us."

He indicated the far side of the street. Walking along parallel to them was Gradey, a Winchester cocked threateningly in his arms. Leif took in the situation and grinned meaninglessly again. The trail-hand had probably not intended making a move for the money yet anyway, thought Prayer. He would choose a better time and place than this.

"When do we get our share, Mr Jericho?" enquired Leif, with mock respect.

"I'll be paying off in the saloon in ten minutes," said Jericho shortly. "You can wait for me there."

"Yes, sir, Mr Jericho, anything you say!" said the trail-hand.

Leif touched the brim of his stetson with exaggerated courtesy and swaggered off down the street with the other cowhands in close attendance. Reluctantly the townsfolk made way for them.

"Come on," said Jericho impatiently. "We don't want to run our luck into the ground."

The three of them reached the bank through the scowling, hostile crowds without incident. It was oddly quiet now that the lowing of the steers in the stockyard could no longer be heard.

Brannigan was waiting for them

inside the bank. Jericho put his canvas bag down on a table and signalled to Prayer to do the same with his. The rancher opened one of the grips and took out a handful of notes with which to pay the trail herders. Then he handed both bags over to Brannigan.

"Let's see this strong-room of yours," he said curtly.

Without a word the bank owner walked over to a steel door with a narrow grill and with an effort pushed it open.

"There," he said.

Jericho nodded. "I'll just be keeping it here overnight," he said. "Give me a receipt."

Brannigan moved in a stately fashion to his desk and scribbled a receipt, which he handed over to the rancher. Jericho folded the paper carefully and put it in his pocket. He indicated Prayer and Gradey.

"My two men will be on guard outside," he said.

"As you wish," said Brannigan stiffly.

The bank owner picked up the two canvas grips with an effort and deposited them both in the strong-room. He locked the gate with a key and turned enquiringly to Jericho.

"Will that be all?" he enquired.

"For the time being," answered the rancher.

The four men left the bank. Without a word to the others Brannigan locked the front door and walked away down the still crowded street.

"You two keep an eye on this place," said Jericho. "I'll go and pay off the hands."

Jericho left for the saloon. Prayer looked at Gradey as the two men stood on the boardwalk outside the bank. The crowds in the street regarded them both with interest. Already rumours as to the extent of the fortune just placed in the bank were circulating freely. The most common estimate was that fifty thousand dollars had been placed in the strong-room for safe keeping.

"Might as well make ourselves

comfortable," said Gradey, sprawling on the boardwalk with his back against the wall. Prayer perched less comfortably on the hitching-rail in front of the bank. Mayor Ellcott thrust his way to the front of the ogling crowd.

"Are you two expecting trouble here?" he demanded.

Gradey shrugged and did not respond. Prayer got down from the hitching-rail.

"Hard to say, Mr Ellcott," he said respectfully. "I've been hired to protect Mr Jericho's deposit in the bank until tomorrow morning."

"But are you expecting an attempt to be made to steal that money?" persisted the mayor.

The crowd fell silent as its members craned forward to hear Prayer's reply.

"It's a lot of money," said Prayer.

"Quite so," said Ellcott. "And I'm sure we don't need telling who it is who might make an attempt to steal it. The same Union sympathisers who raided this town and who have been raising merry hell in its streets. Well, I am here to tell you, John Prayer, that we are united against those Northerners in Trail's End, and any help you need will be forthcoming from the citizens of this town."

An enthusiastic cheer went up from the street. Ellcott puffed himself up with pride and made as if to say something else. Before he could do so there was an angry cry from the far end of the street.

Prayer looked over the heads of the crowd. Pa Kennedy was riding towards the bank. He was leading another horse. On its back was Kate, looking mortified.

"You've found Kate!" declared Mayor Ellcott. "Where was she? Who was it who kidnapped her?"

"Hell, she was never kidnapped," snorted the saloon owner in disgust. "I was riding past Prayer's place just now and I saw somebody moving about inside. I knew that Prayer was with Jericho, so I went inside and found

Miss Kate there. If you asked me she's been there all the time, just making on that she was kidnapped!"

An angry growl went up from the people in the street. Kate flinched. Mayor Ellcott looked bewildered.

"Is this true?" he asked Prayer. "Do you mean that Kate was never kidnapped by the trail-herders at all? But why did you pretend that she was?"

"Hell, ain't it obvious?" asked Pa Kennedy. "They're both in this with Jericho and the trail-herders. They're all in this together."

"Is that true?" asked Ellcott.

"Of course it's true," said Pa Kennedy. "All you've got to do is look at their faces."

Desperately Prayer tried to think of something to say which would explain properly what had happened. The words would not come, while Kate looked too frightened to speak.

"So it was all some sort of a fraud," sighed Ellcott. "I'm disappointed, John.

It was bad enough you working with the trail-herders. I didn't think you'd try to trick the town as well."

The mayor's sentiments were echoed in the angry cries coming from the crowd. Ellcott fought the shouts down and obtained some sort of order. Then he fumed back to Prayer.

"I don't know what's going on here, and I don't care," he said. "All I know is that the decent people of this town don't have any more regard for you, Prayer. If anything happens now, you're on your own!"

13

"WHEN do you think they'll come?" asked Prayer quietly. Wade Jericho shook his head. "Can't rightly say," he shrugged. "But they'll be here. Depend on it."

The two men were standing on the boardwalk outside the bank in the twilight. Gradey was standing a few yards from them, looking up and down the otherwise deserted street. It was very quiet now that the cattle-train had left and the crowds had broken up and dispersed.

The three men had piled up as many barriers as possible between the front door of the bank and the street, leaving just enough room for them to crouch behind the obstacles. There was an upturned table and four armchairs, which they had obtained from Kate after Prayer had escorted her back to the boarding house, and several mattresses which Gradey had appeared with after a scouting mission down several side alleys.

More obstacles in the shape of bales of hay taken from the livery table had been placed on the flat roof of the bank. The bank building was taller than the others in the street, so it could not be overlooked by any of the neighbouring stores. The hay bales were so placed that a man lying behind them would have a good view of anyone trying to approach the bank from the back or sides.

"There's no way they can get in, except through the door at the front," Jericho had pointed out to the other two, "but they may try to get round behind us. That's why one of us is going to have to go up on the roof."

That had been over an hour ago, when the trail-boss had returned from paying off the cowhands in the saloon. Shortly afterwards they had seen Billy Leif and the others riding out of town.

Jericho had listened without expression when Prayer had explained that the townsfolk no longer had any intention of coming to their aid if the herders raided the bank.

"Can't be helped," he had said finally. "There's still the three of us. You and me will take the front. Gradey will watch the back and sides from the roof."

"Three of us against ten of them," said Prayer.

"Nobody said it was going to be an easy way of making fifty dollars," Jericho had told him.

Men had started drifting into the saloon from early evening in a strange, unformulated desire for company and the strength that came from being together in a crisis. By nine o'clock the place was packed. For the most part the drinkers sat in an uneasy silence. Even Mayor Ellcott abandoned his usual table-hopping glad-handing in search of votes and was nursing his beer morosely.

Pa Kennedy came over to the mayor, ignoring repeated requests for drinks from barflies. The saloon-owner leaned across the bar and thrust his unshaven face close to Ellcott's.

"If you're worried about the bank, forget it," he wheezed. "These days there ain't above a few cents in it belonging to the town."

"The way I heard it, Wade Jericho put in more than thirty-five thousand dollars this afternoon."

"Hell, that's Jericho's money. Don't mean a thing to us. He's paying the 'breed and John Prayer to guard it for him."

"The talk is," said Ellcott worriedly, "that Jericho reckons his cowhands are going to raid the bank tonight."

"So what?" asked the saloon-owner indifferently. "Let 'em kill one another, I say."

"It may be Jericho's money," said Ellcott defiantly, "but it's the town's bank."

Pa Kennedy stared blankly at the

236

mayor. "What the hell has got to do with anything?" he asked.

"You wouldn't begin to understand," said Mayor Ellcott with a spirit which he had not displayed for many years.

The attack came shortly after midnight. Leif and the trail-hands came whooping up the main street, their Colts in their hands, convinced that there would be no opposition from the townsfolk and that the three men guarding the bank would not be able long to withstand an onslaught from ten experienced gunslingers. They rode into a fight that was to be talked about in Kansas for years to come.

Jericho and Prayer crouched waiting behind their makeshift barricades, while on the roof of the bank Gradey sprawled at full length, cradling his Winchester affectionately in his arms.

"Let 'em have it!" snarled Jericho when the outlaws were within range.

The three men pumped lead at the attacking horsemen, bringing down two of the trail-hands in the first volley.

However, despite the ferocity and accuracy of their fire, they could not prevent Leif and the other survivors from diving from their mounts and scurrying to take up positions on the boardwalk opposite the bank, and returning the fire with interest.

Prayer concentrated on directing his fire into the dark doorway of the grain store opposite the bank, where he had seen two of the trail-hands diving hastily for cover. He heard a sharp cry which indicated that he had hit one of the men, but a steady fusillade continued to spit from the doorway in his direction, indicating that he had only winged the outlaw.

To his left Jericho was firing with two heavy Colts alternately, grunting with the effort of bringing the cumbersome weapons to bear, but not letting his concentration waver for one second. From above they could hear the steady barking of Gradey's Winchester as the half-breed directed his fire down on the street from the roof.

For ten minutes the defenders put up a spirited battle from behind their barricades, but in the dark Leif and the trail-herders were able constantly to adjust their positions, running and crawling to a number of vantage points surrounding the bank building. Shots were pouring in on the defenders from all angles, riddling the facade of the bank.

Gradey was the first to be hit. An outlaw armed with a rifle had managed to secure a position from a window in the second storey of a building across the street. He pumped six rapid shots through the bale of hay behind which the half-breed was concealed. Gradey gave a sharp cry and lay still.

"Where the hell do you think you're going?" snapped Jericho as Prayer edged back from his position and cast an assessing eye at the front of the bank.

"They've got Gradey," Prayer answered. "I'll try to get up to him."

"Don't be a damned fool," rumbled

Jericho. "You try and climb up there and they'll pick you off like a fly."

"We ain't going to be able to stay here much longer," pointed out Prayer. "They've got us pinned down."

"I'd worked that out for myself," grunted the other man. "Cover me. I'll try and flush a couple of 'em out."

Before Prayer could stop him the big rancher rose and walked slowly out into the street.

"All right Leif," he called. "Stop hiding in the dark like a whipped dog. Come out and face me like a man!"

Three shots cracked out from the darkness of the night and Jericho staggered backwards. Before he fell he loosed off a shot in the direction of one of the reports. There was the crash of a body tumbling from a window to the street below. Then Jericho twisted and fell to the ground. From his position on the boardwalk Prayer fired in the direction of another of the flashes from the other side of the street. He heard another man fall.

They had probably killed two more of the outlaws but now he was on his own.

There was a silence in the street for a minute. Then Leif's voice echoed across the gloom.

"Prayer, can you hear me?"

"I hear you," replied Prayer cautiously.

"We've got Jericho and the 'breed. There's only you left."

"Ain't got so many yourself, Leif. How many have we gunned down so far? I make it four or five. Maybe more."

"Never mind that. We got enough to take you."

"You've still got to get across the street. Reckon I can bring down three more before you reach the bank, once you show yourselves."

There was another pause. Then Leif called out again, in a would-be conciliatory tone.

"Ain't no need for that, Prayer. We got no quarrel with you. You ain't the marshal no more. No need to

241

get yourself killed protecting a bank that belongs to somebody else. And anything Jericho paid you you've more than earned these last few minutes."

"What's your point, Leif?" asked Prayer, peering through the darkness to make sure that the outlaw was not trying to distract him while other men crawled across the street.

"Ride away," came the immediate response. "Get on your horse and ride out of town. We'll give you five minutes. Then we'll come across and take the bank. By that time you'll be long gone. Come on, you don't owe the town a damn thing, the way you've been treated."

Prayer considered the offer. Leif probably meant it. It would be worth the outlaw's while to let him escape in the dark to prevent further resistance And the other man certainly had a point about his owing the town nothing. All the same, Prayer knew what he was going to do.

"Well?" came the impatient demand

from across the street. "How about it, Prayer?"

"Sorry, Leif," said Prayer brusquely. "It wouldn't be right letting you cross the street just like that."

He heard the outlaw curse vehemently and then the shots started crashing into the front of the bank building again. Prayer did his best to fire back, but he knew that he was making little impact upon the superior numbers opposite and that it was only a matter of minutes before the trail-herders tried to rush him.

The occupants of the crowded saloon gave up all pretence of drinking and whirled round to face the door as Doc Emblem rushed in from the street.

"You crazy old galoot, you could have got yourself killed," muttered Pa Kennedy. "What you been doing outside with all that firing going on?"

"Cause I'm a nosy crazy old galoot," said the doctor defiantly. "I wanted to know what was going on."

"Well, what is going on?" demanded Mayor Ellcott.

"Jericho's down," the old doctor informed them breathlessly. "So is the 'breed. There's only Prayer left. They offered to let him ride out if he'd give up the bank. Said it was none of his business to guard it, seeing as he wasn't our marshal no more."

"What did Prayer say to that?" asked Kennedy uneasily.

"Told 'em to try and take it from him."

The men in the saloon fell silent as they digested the latest information. Ellcott took a long drink from his glass. Then he raised it again and drained it to the dregs. He sat in unhappy contemplation for a moment. Then he stood up. All eyes in the saloon were on the mayor.

"That does it," he said to no one in particular.

"What do you mean?" asked Pa Kennedy in an alarmed tone.

"I mean that I'm fed up with hiding

behind other men. We had to rely on Tod Washburn to lead us against the Night Riders. Now we're letting John Prayer defend our bank for us. The Lord knows I ain't no fighter, and right now I'm as scared as hell, but I can fire a gun. I'm going out to give John Prayer a hand, for what it's worth."

The mayor strode across the room, taking his revolver from its holster with a trembling hand as he did so. At the door he turned and faced the sea of faces gaping uncertainly before him.

"The rest of you can do what you think best," he said shortly.

Prayer strained his eyes through the gloom. The five minutes allowed him by Billy Leif had passed. The outlaws should be making their rush at any moment.

He caught a brief glimpse of a movement on the other side of the street and fired twice from behind the mattress he was using as a shelter. He thought he heard one of the trail-hands fall and then the rest of them were rushing across the intervening space at him, firing wildly.

Shots thudded all around him. Prayer fired back without taking aim. The shadows of the running men were half-way across the street now. He braced himself for the pain which would come as they shot him down in their headlong advance.

Suddenly a heavier fusillade of shots swept across the street, ripping into the bodies of the outlaws caught in a cross-fire. Leif and the others cried out in surprise and pain. One by one their bodies went crashing to the ground and lay still. Still the shots thudded into their lifeless corpses, making them twitch in a grotesque dance of death. Then the shots died away.

Slowly Prayer rose to his feet and advanced into the street, wondering if he was taking part in some wound inflicted fantasy. He looked down at the bodies of six outlaws sprawled before him. Then he looked up to see Mayor Ellcott and Doc Emblem at the head of about twenty assorted men from the saloon. They all bore smoking guns and were looking down with mingled awe and satisfaction at the bodies of the outlaws. They had taken the cowhands by surprise and overwhelmed them by sheer firepower.

"Sorry we were late, John," said Ellcott awkwardly.

Prayer shook his head slowly. "Far as I'm concerned Mayor Ellcott, you timed it just fine," he said faintly.

14

THE whistle of the first passenger train to visit the town screamed impatiently as it gathered a head of steam to pull out of Trail's End on its return journey to Chicago. Wade Jericho offered his hand to John Prayer and Mayor Ellcott. In spite of himself he winced from the pain of his heavily bandaged left leg.

"Time to go," said the rancher. "I want to say thank you for everything."

A month had passed since the citizens of the town had come to the aid of John Prayer in his defence of the bank. The life of the town had returned to normal, except for the extra graves on Boot Hill of Billy Leif and the other outlaws slain outside the bank. After the night gun fight in the main street Doc Emblem had announced with some surprise that both Jericho and Gradey were still alive, and had done his best to patch them up. Now the two men were on their way by train to Chicago for more medical treatment. Gradey, as impassive as ever, was clutching a saddlebag containing some of the money obtained from the sale of the herd.

"I've left a fair sum in the town bank," said Jericho, staring meaningfully at the silver star back in place on Prayer's chest. "Take care of it for me, Marshal."

"Hell," said Mayor Ellcott boastfully. "There ain't an outlaw in the west who'll go up against the bank at Trail's End. Not after what happened last month."

"They may be right at that," acknowledged Jericho. "You surely earned yourself a reputation as a law town that night. They're already calling you and your sidekicks Ellcott's Vigilantes. Wouldn't be surprised if Ned Buntline didn't write one of his books about you, Mayor." He stepped with an effort on to the train, followed by Gradey, and looked down at the mayor and the marshal.

"I underestimated you, Mayor Ellcott," he admitted. "You saved the three of us raising that posse in the saloon and coming out the way you did, with us outgunned."

Ellcott shuddered. "I can tell you one thing," he said with candour and utter conviction. "As long as I live I ain't never going to do anything brave on purpose again." A slow grin creased his face and he puffed out his meagre chest. "On the other hand, I reckon I ain't never going to have to kiss no babies for votes no more neither. I estimate I'm a shoe-in for mayor on the law-and-order ticket for as long as I care to run."

"You'll have my vote," promised the rancher gravely. He turned to Prayer. "Soon as I'm fixed up I'm going to drive a bigger herd to Trail's End," he said. "I'm fixing to bring in two drives a year from now on. Bought me a parcel of property hereabouts as well.

If the town's going to grow I want to grow with it. So take care of my town, John Prayer."

"So long as you bring real trail-hands, not outlaws, with you next time, you'll be welcome," smiled Prayer.

The train started steaming out of the station. Jericho waved back at them from the observation car until it was out of sight. Ellcott looked hopefully at Prayer.

"Do you think he meant it when he said they might write a book about me?" he asked.

"Hell, Mayor," said Prayer with a straight face. "They've already written about Wild Bill Hickock and Buffalo Bill Cody. Who's left to write about but you?"

"That's right," said Ellcott with rising excitement. He stopped and stared suspiciously at Prayer. "You wouldn't be joshing me, would you?" he asked.

"Would I do a thing like that, Mayor Ellcott?"

"No, I guess not." The mayor

frowned at another thought. "I didn't like it when Jericho called Trail's End his town just now," he said.

"Don't give it another thought," said the marshal confidently. He started to head purposefully for the boarding house and Kate. Half-way across the street he looked back over his shoulder at the other man.

"It's our town, too," he said.

THE END

FIGHTING RAMROD
Charles N. Heckelmann

Most men would have cut their losses, but Frazer counted the bullets in his guns and said he'd soak the range in blood before he'd give up another inch of what was his.

LONE GUN
Eric Allen

Smoke Blackbird had been away too long. The Lequires had seized the Blackbird farm, forcing the Indians and settlers off, and no one seemed willing to fight! He had to fight alone.

THE THIRD RIDER
Barry Cord

Mel Rawlins wasn't going to let anything stand in his way. His father was murdered, his two brothers gone. Now Mel rode for vengeance.

ARIZONA DRIFTERS
W. C. Tuttle

When drifting Dutton and Lonnie Steelman decide to become partners they find that they have a common enemy in the formidable Thurston brothers.

TOMBSTONE
Matt Braun

Wells Fargo paid Luke Starbuck to outgun the silver-thieving stagecoach gang at Tombstone. Before long Luke can see the only thing bearing fruit in this eldorado will be the gallows tree.

HIGH BORDER RIDERS
Lee Floren

Buckshot McKee and Tortilla Joe cut the trail of a border tough who was running Mexican beef into Texas. They stopped the smuggler in his tracks.

BRETT RANDALL, GAMBLER
E. B. Mann

Larry Day had the choice of running away from the law or of assuming a dead man's place. No matter what he decided he was bound to end up dead.

THE GUNSHARP
William R. Cox

The Eggerleys weren't very smart. They trained their sights on Will Carney and Arizona's biggest blood bath began.

THE DEPUTY OF SAN RIANO
Lawrence A. Keating and
Al. P. Nelson

When a man fell dead from his horse, Ed Grant was spotted riding away from the scene. The deputy sheriff rode out after him and came up against everything from gunfire to dynamite.

FARGO: MASSACRE RIVER
John Benteen

The ambushers up ahead had now blocked the road. Fargo's convoy was a jumble, a perfect target for the insurgents' weapons!

SUNDANCE: DEATH IN THE LAVA
John Benteen

The Modoc's captured the wagon train and its cargo of gold. But now the halfbreed they called Sundance was going after it . . .

HARSH RECKONING
Phil Ketchum

Five years of keeping himself alive in a brutal prison had made Brand tough and careless about who he gunned down . . .

FARGO: PANAMA GOLD
John Benteen

With foreign money behind him, Buckner was going to destroy the Panama Canal before it could be completed. Fargo's job was to stop Buckner.

FARGO: THE SHARPSHOOTERS
John Benteen

The Canfield clan, thirty strong were raising hell in Texas. Fargo was tough enough to hold his own against the whole clan.

PISTOL LAW
Paul Evan Lehman

Lance Jones came back to Mustang for just one thing — revenge! Revenge on the people who had him thrown in jail.

HELL RIDERS
Steve Mensing

Wade Walker's kid brother, Duane, was locked up in the Silver City jail facing a rope at dawn. Wade was a ruthless outlaw, but he was smart, and he had vowed to have his brother out of jail before morning!

DESERT OF THE DAMNED
Nelson Nye

The law was after him for the murder of a marshal — a murder he didn't commit. Breen was after him for revenge — and Breen wouldn't stop at anything . . . blackmail, a frameup . . . or murder.

DAY OF THE COMANCHEROS
Steven C. Lawrence

Their very name struck terror into men's hearts — the Comancheros, a savage army of cutthroats who swept across Texas, leaving behind a bloodstained trail of robbery and murder.

SUNDANCE: SILENT ENEMY
John Benteen

A lone crazed Cheyenne was on a personal war path. They needed to pit one man against one crazed Indian. That man was Sundance.

LASSITER
Jack Slade

Lassiter wasn't the kind of man to listen to reason. Cross him once and he'll hold a grudge for years to come — if he let you live that long.

LAST STAGE TO GOMORRAH
Barry Cord

Jeff Carter, tough ex-riverboat gambler, now had himself a horse ranch that kept him free from gunfights and card games. Until Sturvesant of Wells Fargo showed up.

McALLISTER ON THE COMANCHE CROSSING
Matt Chisholm

The Comanche, McAllister owes them a life — and the trail is soaked with the blood of the men who had tried to outrun them before.

QUICK-TRIGGER COUNTRY
Clem Colt

Turkey Red hooked up with Curly Bill Graham's outlaw crew. But wholesale murder was out of Turk's line, so when range war flared he bucked the whole border gang alone . . .

CAMPAIGNING
Jim Miller

Ambushed on the Santa Fe trail, Sean Callahan is saved by two Indian strangers. But there'll be more lead and arrows flying before the band join Kit Carson against the Comanches.

GUNSLINGER'S RANGE
Jackson Cole

Three escaped convicts are out for revenge. They won't rest until they put a bullet through the head of the dirty snake who locked them behind bars.

RUSTLER'S TRAIL
Lee Floren

Jim Carlin knew he would have to stand up and fight because he had staked his claim right in the middle of Big Ike Outland's best grass.

THE TRUTH ABOUT SNAKE RIDGE
Marshall Grover

The troubleshooters came to San Cristobal to help the needy. For Larry and Stretch the turmoil began with a brawl and then an ambush.

WOLF DOG RANGE
Lee Floren

Will Ardery would stop at nothing, unless something stopped him first — like a bullet from Pete Manly's gun.

DEVIL'S DINERO
Marshall Grover

Plagued by remorse, a rich old reprobate hired the Texas Trouble-shooters to deliver a fortune in greenbacks to each of his victims.

GUNS OF FURY
Ernest Haycox

Dane Starr, alias Dan Smith, wanted to close the door on his past and hang up his guns, but people wouldn't let him.

DONOVAN
Elmer Kelton

Donovan was supposed to be dead. Uncle Joe Vickers had fired off both barrels of a shotgun into the vicious outlaw's face as he was escaping from jail. Now Uncle Joe had been shot — in just the same way.

CODE OF THE GUN
Gordon D. Shirreffs

MacLean came riding home, with saddle tramp written all over him, but sewn in his shirt-lining was an Arizona Ranger's star.

GAMBLER'S GUN LUCK
Brett Austen

Gamblers seldom live long. Parker was a hell of a gambler. It was his life — or his death . . .

ORPHAN'S PREFERRED
Jim Miller

Sean Callahan answers the call of the Pony Express and fights Indians and outlaws to get the mail through.

DAY OF THE BUZZARD
T. V. Olsen

All Val Penmark cared about was getting the men who killed his wife.

THE MANHUNTER
Gordon D. Shirreffs

Lee Kershaw knew that every Rurale in the territory was on the lookout for him. But the offer of $5,000 in gold to find five small pieces of leather was too good to turn down.

RIFLES ON THE RANGE
Lee Floren

Doc Mike and the farmer stood there alone between Smith and Watson. There was this moment of stillness, and then the roar would start. And somebody would die . . .

HARTIGAN
Marshall Grover

Hartigan had come to Cornerstone to die. He chose the time and the place, and Main Street became a battlefield.

SUNDANCE: OVERKILL
John Benteen

When a wealthy banker's daughter was kidnapped by the Cheyenne, he offered Sundance $10,000 to rescue the girl.